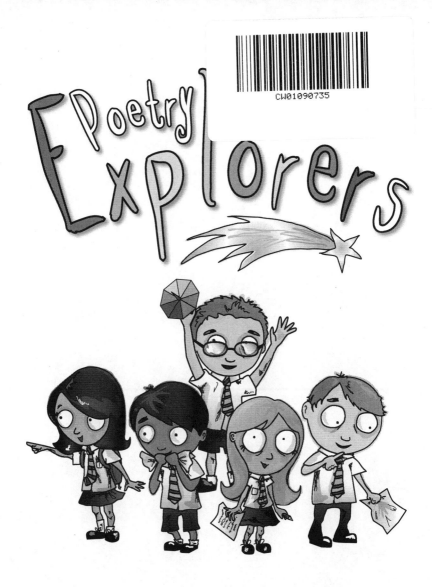

Poetry Explorers

Poems From Southern Scotland

Edited by Lisa Adlam

First published in Great Britain in 2009 by

 Young**Writers**

Remus House
Coltsfoot Drive
Peterborough
PE2 9JX
Telephone: 01733 890066
Website: www.youngwriters.co.uk

Foreword

At Young Writers our defining aim is to promote an enjoyment of reading and writing amongst children and young adults. By giving aspiring poets the opportunity to see their work in print, their love of the written word as well as confidence in their own abilities has the chance to blossom.

Our latest competition Poetry Explorers was designed to introduce primary school children to the wonders of creative expression. They were given free reign to write on any theme and in any style, thus encouraging them to use and explore a variety of different poetic forms.

We are proud to present the resulting collection of regional anthologies which are an excellent showcase of young writing talent. With such a diverse range of entries received, the selection process was difficult yet very rewarding. From comical rhymes to poignant verses, there is plenty to entertain and inspire within these pages. We hope you agree that this collection bursting with imagination is one to treasure.

Contents

St Columba's Primary School, Cupar

St Leonard's School, St Andrews

St Patrick's Primary School, Greenock

St Peter's RC Primary School, Edinburgh

Sheuchan Primary School, Stranraer

Sinclairtoun Primary School, Kirkcaldy

The Poems

School Work

School work, school work every day,
When will I get time to play?

Catch the bus, don't be late,
My friends are waiting by the gate.
Every day at nine o'clock,
All the fun has to stop.

My first lesson in the class,
Always is that dreaded maths,
Division, addition and subtraction,
What a complete and utter distraction!

This I really should not mention,
But I find it hard to pay attention,
When my thoughts want to stray,
To having fun and games to play.

Now it's time for that English language,
Oh, my tummy's rumbling, for my salad sandwich!
But all is not bad,
There's some fun to be had,
It's time for PE,
We can run wild and be free!

Shhh! I can hear the school bells chime,
Hooray, at last it's finally home time!

School work, school work every day,
Now's my chance to go and play!

Victoria Barclay (10)
Alexandra Primary School, Airdrie

Dance With Your Soul

Don't dance with your feet,
Dance with your soul.
I would love to win a trophy,
It's my lifetime goal!

Arms in Braba,
Feet in first,
Remember to smile,
Don't make this worse!

The curtains open,
It's time for the show,
In a red satin dress,
The music starts to flow!

I start to dance,
I'm shaky inside,
But I love to dance,
It's a fact I can't hide!

The music stops,
I take a bow,
I feel great inside,
But the dance is over now!

Shannon Smith (11)
Alexandra Primary School, Airdrie

Friends!

Friends are forever
You're never seen apart
They're always very special to you
And have a special place in your heart.

Wherever you go on holiday
To Paris, Madrid or Rome
They'll always be there waiting for you
Whenever you come home!

Even if it's raining
Or sunny or sleet or snow
Your friends will always be there for you
Whatever the weather shows.

If you're going out shopping
Or going for a walk
Your friends will always be there for you
If you ever need to talk.

Be glad that you have friends
That are really special to you
And if you're really nice to them
You'll be special to them too!

Amy Carroll (11)
Alexandra Primary School, Airdrie

Outer Space

I left the Earth one day
And I didn't know what to say.
Before I knew it, my rocket had flew it,
Up to a place far away!

No gravity around,
My feet are no longer on the ground.
Flying in the air,
Without any time to spare.

Whooshing around in my big red rocket,
It's such fun, I never want to stop it!
I wish I could do this every day,
But unfortunately I cannot stay!

I'd better go home now for my dinner,
I wish I could stay in space forever.
It's been great fun being an astronaut for the day,
Now I can tell all my friends when I go out to play!

Sheryl O'Hare (11)
Alexandra Primary School, Airdrie

The Ocean

O pen and always goes on
C lams lying at the bottom of the sea, waiting for divers to discover them
E normous whales and dolphins passing by
A nd sharks never lose their appetite by feeding on fish
N ever ends.

Matthew Robertson (10)
Alexandra Primary School, Airdrie

My Hobbies

I have lots of hobbies, I bet you do too,
I am going to share some of mine with you.
Dancing is my favourite of all,
Or maybe even shopping at the mall.

I love to read exciting books,
Or try out some funky new looks.
Playing badminton is so great,
Or hanging out with a mate!

Going to school isn't so cool,
But tennis and swimming totally rule.
Playing outside with my friends,
We hope fun times never end!

I also love to play netball,
Even though I'm not that tall.
I have told you everything I love to do,
So now you can have fun too!

Hannah Roche (11)
Alexandra Primary School, Airdrie

Chess

C hess is a thinking game
H ard to learn, but it gets easier
E veryone can join, beginners and professionals
S ometimes you're victorious and sometimes you lose
S o if you still want to play chess, join a chess club.

Bart Waszkiewicz (10)
Alexandra Primary School, Airdrie

Space Life Up Above

S atellites roaming around looking for new planets
P luto getting smaller every year
A stronauts bouncing at zero gravity
C onstellations everywhere in sight
E clipses don't happen very often

L unar light shining upon you
I n with the never-ending fun beyond Earth
F inding something new above the clouds
E arth so small compared to Jupiter

U ranus glowing blue from afar
P lanets look so great up there

A stronomers keep finding new moons on Saturn
B ig Bang 14 billions years ago still so famous!
O nly 93,000,000 miles from the sun!
V enus takes 255 days to revolve around the sun!
E arth is made up of two thirds water.

Paula Glen (10)

Alexandra Primary School, Airdrie

Grizzly Bear

Brown hair,
Sharp teeth,
Speedy runner,
Sad eyed.

Cute cubs,
Hibernator,
Salmon catcher,
Circus dancer.

Massive paws,
Scary claws,
Shaggy fur,
Water lover.

River paddler,
Wet noses,
Strong legs,
Not friendly.

Erin Dearie (10)
Alexandra Primary School, Airdrie

Volcanoes

V olcanologists running away from a lava flow
O minous bulge growing on the side of an active volcano like
   Mount St Helens
L ahars - giant rivers of mud sliding down like a bulldozer
   and destroying everything in their path
C ertain death
A ctive volcanoes like Mauna Loa are lovely to look at, but are
   very deadly
N ot all volcanoes are active, like Kilamanjaro in Africa
O n an active volcano, you might want to put on a gas mask
E ruptions more powerful than hundreds of nuclear bombs
   like Mount Vesuvius in Italy
S ome volcanoes are in space and underwater, like Olympus Mons
   on Mars. It is the biggest in the universe.

Leo Reilly (10)
Alexandra Primary School, Airdrie

Football

I love football because, well it's football,
I like the noise of people when they score,
I love the sound of the ball being kicked,
I like my team winning a game,
I love it when I do all my tricks,
I like it when I skin everybody,
I also love it when we win a game,
I like the round ball shape,
I love my favourite teams, Celtic and Scotland,
Best of all, I love the team I play for.

Rhiannan Brown (10)
Alexandra Primary School, Airdrie

Irish Dancing

I rish dancing makes you fit and more flexible
R eady, set, go! To the competition they go
I reland is the place they travel to most
S hoes and wigs are a lot of fun
H eavy shoes and pumps are the shoes they wear

D resses are the best of all
A ll the time you meet new friends
N ever give up, always try again
C old or hot, they still dance a lot
I t is very fun and enjoyable
N ever get upset if you do not win, be happy for the ones that do
G lamour is fun, but winning is better.

Sophie McLelland (10)
Alexandra Primary School, Airdrie

Animals

Dogs are cute,
Frogs are not,
Dogs play with rope tied in a knot,
Hedgehogs are really spiky,
If I had a dog, it would be called Mikey.

Cats chase rats,
Rats run around,
The cat sneaks up without a sound,
Bats sleep during the day and wake at night,
And fly about without a doubt.

Caitlin Lambie (10)
Alexandra Primary School, Airdrie

Ice Skating

I ce skating rocks, it is my favourite thing to do
C ool and cold
E xcellent fun for everyone

S kating with friends, what I love to do
K een to try new tricks
A t the rink shivering with nerves
T rying my best to beat the rest
I ce skating is the hobby I like best
N ever want to come off, I could stay on all day
G liding on the ice like a graceful swan.

Megan Kay (11)
Alexandra Primary School, Airdrie

Outer Space

O rbiting around the sun, all nine planets
U ri Gagarin, the first man in space
T ransmitting information back to Earth
E arth, a planet we must embrace
R ocks make up Mars, the red planet

S un, the ball that gives us light
P luto is the smallest planet
A ll the time on Neptune it's always night
C rash! A sad ending for Apollo 13
E clipses make it not so bright.

David Lowe (10)
Alexandra Primary School, Airdrie

My Dog

Nose-sniffer
Leg-mover
Paw-licker
Tongue-sweater
Shoe-stealer
Sock-chewer
Noisy-barker
Tail-wagger
Owner-lover
A great pal.

Sean Goodall (11)
Alexandra Primary School, Airdrie

Drama Poem

D rama is fun because you put on shows
R esting your voice so you sing well
A ll you do is games and have lots of fun
M ama Mia could be the show, who knows?
A fter shows you have a party, so come along and join in

P lays are sometimes what you also do
O n stage you get nervous with a sore tummy
E xcitement is what you get before you perform
M ime is something you act out without speaking.

Philip McBride (11)
Alexandra Primary School, Airdrie

The Dark, Scary Forest

Three boys out today,
Off they go away to play.
In the forest calls Jay to play,
So, in they go with their ball,
It's getting dark at nightfall.

There were branches snapping,
Owls hooting, foxes running,
The forest was so scary when the wildlife came out,
The three boys ran home.

Leon Hillen (10)

Alexandra Primary School, Airdrie

Football Game

F un and joy, that is the feeling
O ut and about with our friends
O verall, football brings out the best in everyone
T elevision is nothing like the atmosphere - it is sensational
B eckham and Ronaldo are my favourite players
A ction-packed games are the best
L ove football, it is my favourite sport
L et football be your best friend.

Sam Watson (11)

Alexandra Primary School, Airdrie

My Feelings

F unny I can sometimes be
E veryone might not think I am
E veryone else might
L aughing I might do a lot
I ncredible I may be
N asty is a never for me
G reat is my favourite
S ad is a maybe for me, but not a lot.

Darcie McMurray (10)
Alexandra Primary School, Airdrie

Sunshine

S unshine beating through our windowpanes
U p we jump and shout hooray!
N o time to spare, it's hot out there
S unshine skies shine all day
H appy voices sing and play
I love swimming in the open air
N ever forget to cover up and take care
E xcitement for what tomorrow might bring!

Claudia Conreno (10)
Alexandra Primary School, Airdrie

Doctor Who

Time traveller
TARDIS user
Good fighter
Fast talker
Martha Jones lover
Alien fighter
Rose Tyler lover
Sonic screwdriver user
Alien attacker
Star traveller
Earth protector
Suit wearer
Donna Noble lover
Casandra killer.

Jennifer Sinclair (9)
Dundonald Primary School, Dundonald

Space

Big, cold, lonely space
Planets, darkness, stars everywhere
The sun and Saturn make up the place
Big, cold, lonely space

Eight planets in the sky
But one very big one caught my eye
Earth's a big planet
And that's not a lie.

Ross Wylie (9)
Dundonald Primary School, Dundonald

The Sun

Metal melter
Giant star
Full of lava
Space's light
Maker of life
Master of stars
It's the biggest star ever
Biggest star in the whole of space.

Kris Kirkland (9)
Dundonald Primary School, Dundonald

Space

Space
Cool space
Is really dark
You'll need a shuttle
So you won't
Drop, cool
Space.

Brandon Taylor (9)
Dundonald Primary School, Dundonald

Siblings

Siblings
Mums, dads
Aunties, uncles, cousins
All are your family
Your best friends
Grans, grandpas
Family.

Iain Bell (9)

Dundonald Primary School, Dundonald

The Sun

Sun
Bright yellow
Lovely and hot
Planets orbit the sun
It is never
Ever found
Black.

Abigail Charlwood (9)

Dundonald Primary School, Dundonald

Horses

H orses galloping in the field
O h, what a lovely creature it is
R unning here, running there
S ome horses are everywhere
E ven people ride on their backs
S addle up, it's time to go.

Toni Innes (9)
Dundonald Primary School, Dundonald

The Horse — Cinquain

Pure black
Good and helpful
Beautiful and pretty
An animal is really good
Graceful.

Daryl Milby (9)
Dundonald Primary School, Dundonald

My Teacher

I enter my classroom
And look around
Out the window
On the ground
All the colours
So bright and bold
And if you're naughty
You will be told
The teacher enters
A smile on her face
All the children sit
Silent with grace
She works hard
With those young minds
All the children like her
She is so kind
Even when
They leave someday
They'll remember their first teacher
All of the way.

Jade McMorland (11)

Fisherton Primary School, Dunure

Night Sky

The sun goes down
We wait for dawn
The midnight sky
Seems so magical

The stars so bright
Like sparkling lights
The moonlight shimmers
Through the windows

Apollo's belt
Hardly noticeable
We fall asleep
Having dreams so calm

The morning sun
Wakes you up
Then very soon
Sweet dreams come along.

Jennifer Barnes (12)
Fisherton Primary School, Dunure

Murder

M urder is a sad thing
U nderneath lies a terrible person
R evenge is needed
D esire for murder is addictive
E ventually it will burn them inside
R ampaging through the blood is *guilt.*

Kaylum O'Neill
Fisherton Primary School, Dunure

My Rabbits

C heeky and shy
L oves Murphy
O ff like a bullet
V ery fast
E vil Jnr is her nickname
R espectful she is not

M urphy is his name
U ndeniable he is
R eally cute
P lain active
H appy, very, very happy
Y apper because he looks like he is talking too much.

Ben Chapman (9)
Fisherton Primary School, Dunure

Seashore

S eashores are beautiful
E very summer's day I go to this place, this wonderful place
A nger of the sea and the softness of the sand
S ometimes I just sit there all day and watch the water turn into
foam as it hits the sand
H ere is time to leave once more to have sweet dreams all
night long
O n the last day of summer
R ock pools with snapping crabs
E nd of the day, time to say goodbye for the hard winter,
goodbye seashore.

Hayley Tyson (11)
Fisherton Primary School, Dunure

Eastertime!

E aster eggs
A lways fun
S pringtime
T oo many eggs
E very year
R olling eggs down the hill
T ime to eat
I n memory of Jesus
M ilk chocolate
E aster is very joyful.

Adam Shanks (11)
Fisherton Primary School, Dunure

Seaside

S unny, sandy beaches are the place we like to go
E very seaside brings happy joy and fun
A t a very busy seaside you will find an ice cream van, where
     every child is waiting for a cool, tasty treat
S ee all the children playing in the warm, soft sand
I f you are lucky enough, you might see a seal jumping up
     in the sea
D ifferent adventures every time
E very time you visit the seaside, fun and adventures is what
     you find!

Robyn Sneddon (10)
Fisherton Primary School, Dunure

Tiger

Fierce hunter
Meat eater
Swift runner
Stripy killer
Orange fur
Cute cubs
Orange and black stripes
Is what makes a *tiger.*

Leila Gibson (10)
Fisherton Primary School, Dunure

Winter

Winter
Ice, cold
Freezing, skating, blades
Temperature down, how cold it seems
Hat, gloves, scarves
Cocoa, marshmallows
Snow.

Heidi Geyser (11)
Fisherton Primary School, Dunure

Space

S tars everywhere
P lanets circling the sun
A liens destroying everything in sight
C omets shooting past Earth at the speed of light
E arth is one of the planets in the solar system.

Jordan Gribben (9)
Fisherton Primary School, Dunure

Spain

S uperb food and seas
P ure bright sun and lots of noise
A pizza is best in Spain
I think it's excellent
N oisy children having fun.

Zac Lorimer (9)
Fisherton Primary School, Dunure

23

Air Raid

Sitting, eating food
Rationed food
The air raid siren goes off
I freeze - fear, shock, panic
Searchlights on, sirens go off
Engines roar
Ambulances rush
Will I be in there?

My frozen fear melts
I run
In the shelter
It is damp
Dogs howl
Planes overhead
Flying death
A metal plague
Crash, buildings collapse
In the shelter I am safe
Or am I?

Through the danger of the night
The bullets fly
Nothing left to bomb
They leave
The all clear goes
People look
They sob
It is over
Or is it?

Liam Brown (11)

Flora Stevenson Primary School, Edinburgh

Air Raid

Stomp
Stomp
As the heavy warden walks down the lane
That's when everyone feels the pain

Whoosh
Whoosh
As the planes go by
And all you hear is a screech, a cry

Boom
Boom
Down comes a bomb
Hits my town
And we're all gone
All that's left is a smell of smoke.

Isla Melee (10)
Flora Stevenson Primary School, Edinburgh

Blitz

I am walking down the gloomy road,
Suddenly, the ear-blistering sound,
The dogs howl like it's their last.
They're like vultures circling their prey
As they swoop and drop bombs.
They go and the sound stops.
I look around me, it feels safe but I know it's not.
My house has crumbled and my family has gone
And so has the sky because it's covered in black smoke.

Nathan Richards (10)
Flora Stevenson Primary School, Edinburgh

Dinosaurs

Dinosaurs are tall
Dinosaurs are fierce
Dinosaurs are small
Dinosaurs are scary
Dinosaurs are bony
Dinosaurs are wrinkly
Dinosaurs are loud
Dinosaurs have lots of fights
Dinosaurs have teeth as big as a ruler
Dinosaurs eat meat
Dinosaurs eat leaves
Dinosaurs roar like fireworks
Dinosaurs smell like a skunk
Dinosaurs are as big as a mountain.

Ross Kinnaird (8)
Flora Stevenson Primary School, Edinburgh

Snow

Snow is fantasy
Snow is icy
Snow is crunchy
Snow is fun
Snow is sparkling
Snow is soft
Snow is cold
Snow is fluffy.

Isabel Madden (7)
Flora Stevenson Primary School, Edinburgh

Snow

Snow is very fun
Snow is exciting and freezing too
Snow is sparkling and very cold
Snow is icy
Snow is white and very crunchy
Snow is a fantasy
Snow is like a cloud
Snow is soft and lovely
Snow is slushy
Snow is deep
Snow is fantastic
Snow is great
Snow is frosty.

Matthew Bagshaw (7)
Flora Stevenson Primary School, Edinburgh

Air Raid 1942

Eating a meal, a normal evening
Talking 'bout this and that
A sudden roar, a deafening roar
An air raid siren for sure.

Retreat to the shelter, a fast and long run
Danger is near, almost upon us
We're inside our small, cramped shelter.
My mother is crying like a baby!
Soon it stops, it's all over.
It's such a brilliant relief.

Kim Gray (10)
Flora Stevenson Primary School, Edinburgh

I Can See A Dinosaur

I can see a dinosaur looking at me
I can see a dinosaur, I think he wants his tea
I can see a dinosaur looking very hungry
I can see a dinosaur coming to me
I can see a dinosaur, he is very smelly
I can see a dinosaur, he is looking for his tea
I can see a dinosaur, now he is after me
I can see a dinosaur that keeps following me!

Rebecca Jack (7)
Flora Stevenson Primary School, Edinburgh

My Cat

My cat Sylvester
Is a downright pester

She has been in my house
But never with a mouse

She stuffs her face, my cat
Why do you think she's fat?

She has shiny, black fur
And always loves to purr

And if you stop her jaws
She *will* use her paws

When she is asleep
You never hear a peep.

Maurice McKenna (9)
Glenlee Primary School, Hamilton

Florida Poem!

I went away to Florida
There was lots of sunny weather
All my family came too
We all went together

When we finally got there
I went straight to the pool
The sun was beating down on me
But I felt nice and cool

Next we all went to a park
We all went on a ride
We went on a very scary one
I had butterflies inside

The hotel was really awesome
And the beach was very sandy
We went into a sweetie shop
They do sell some great candy.

Jenna Wrisberg (10)
Glenlee Primary School, Hamilton

My Family Poem

My family are always crazy
And my dad is oh, so lazy!

My brother likes a curry
And he's always in a hurry.

My cousin puts on her clothes
And then she likes to pose.

My mum is very nice,
But she doesn't like rice.

My grandad is always groany,
But I don't mind him being so moany.

My gran makes soup in a pot
And I like it such a lot.

Chloe Dougan (11)
Glenlee Primary School, Hamilton

Regan

I have a little brother
He loves my mother

He is a little cutie
When he wears a wee, blue bootie

He is seven months old
And never does as he is told

My little brother is never quiet
And always causes a huge, big riot!

Regan's always happy
When my mum changes his nappy

I love my little brother
I wouldn't change him for another.

Morgan Smith (9)
Glenlee Primary School, Hamilton

My Holiday

When I go on holiday
I jump into the pool
With my little cousin
So that we both look very cool

We both went to McDonald's
To get a nice McFlurry
We couldn't wait to get there
So we both went in a hurry

Then when we had finished
We had lots of fun
Running about and shouting
And playing in the sun.

Caitlin Shearer (10)
Glenlee Primary School, Hamilton

Rugby Poem

I go to rugby,
Sometimes it can be rough,
Even when we get the hang of it,
It still can be dead tough.

When we are warming up,
We always use the ball,
But our coaches always tell us
Not to kick it tall.

When I play a game,
I know I am the best,
When I come out the scrum,
I'm better than the rest!

Grant Wrisberg (10)
Glenlee Primary School, Hamilton

Football Poem

Football's an amazing sport
It's loved throughout the nation
When Hamilton score the winning goal
We have a celebration

It's half-time already
The refs blown his whistle
Hamilton's winning three to two
Against Cali Thistle

After the game is over
The players' boots stink
They all rush to get ready
For a lovely ice-cold drink!

John Henry (10)
Glenlee Primary School, Hamilton

My Mum

My mum is the best
She is so funny
She is better than the rest
Even though she hasn't got a lot of money.

My mum is very tall
She always spoils me rotten
She cuddles me when I fall
And my birthday is not forgotten.

My mum helps me look beautiful
Any problems she can mend
I love my mum so very much
She is really my best friend!

Sophy Scott (9)
Glenlee Primary School, Hamilton

My Mum

My mum spoils me all the time
She cuddles me when I fall
My mum has a huge, big heart
Although she's only small

My mum has long, black hair
And she likes to buy new clothes
When she gets dressed up at night
She likes to strike a pose

My mum's very cool
I think she's the best
Although she can be moody
She's better than all the rest.

Leanne Wilkie (9)
Glenlee Primary School, Hamilton

Light!

Light can bring us joy
It comes and goes away
I know I need to get up
When the sun comes out to play.

At summertime I play and play
It really is good fun
To jump in shadows with my friends
That are made from the sun.

The sun is very bright
I love the sun a lot
It lights the way all day
And it makes me really hot!

Aimee Brown (9)
Glenlee Primary School, Hamilton

Cyprus

I'm on my way to Cyprus
I have to fly in a plane
All my friends are at home
Playing in the rain

I usually go to restaurants
The meals are very good
Cypriots are really nice people
They are never rude!

I like to go scuba diving
I love to lie in the pool
There is even rally driving
Which I think is really cool.

Martin McNab (9)
Glenlee Primary School, Hamilton

Home

When you go into my room
You will see my bed
If you don't watch out
You might bang your head

My living room is lovely
My mam is so lucky
We try not
To get it mucky

My mum's room is so lovely
It could win a prize
With its creamy coloured cupboard
The shock ran up to my eyes.

Kalum Kerr (9)
Glenlee Primary School, Hamilton

Football Team

My football team wins every game
Because we are the best.
We are top of the league
And better than the rest.

My coach is very shouty,
He's bossy and he is frowny.
He tells us if we lose a game,
He'll send us to the Brownies.

We want to reach the final
And lift the silver cup,
We will be the champions
And my coach can just shut up!

Jason McColl (10)
Glenlee Primary School, Hamilton

My Teacher

My teacher is the best
There is no doubt about it
She's better than all the rest
No one else would doubt it!

She is really very clever
At maths, language and more
If we listen carefully
I'm sure our marks will soar!

She sometimes shouts and moans at us
But she's mostly very kind
Although I've had lots of teachers
A nicer one I couldn't find!

Briony Gray (10)
Glenlee Primary School, Hamilton

GoGos

GoGos are really cool
But some look like fools

Some are fat
And wear a hat

GoGos are really cool
But some look like fools

One looks silly
And I call it Billy

GoGos are really cool
But some look like fools.

Starien Bradley (10)
Glenlee Primary School, Hamilton

WWI

Black smoke
Sopwith biplanes
Guns firing
Focker triplanes
SE5s flying
Propellers spinning
Dusty runways
Uncomfortable seats
Hurricanes landing
Raging fires
Red Baron
Red Baron intercepted.

Jordan Bell (9)
Kennoway Primary & Community School, Kennoway

Kennings – My Dog

Stick catcher
Treat begger
Lead puller
Brown Lab
Mud trailer
Soft fur
Shower hater
Food lover
Long walker
Fast runner
A cute little puppy.

Laurie Seath (9)
Kennoway Primary & Community School, Kennoway

Kennings – Rabbit

Carrot muncher
Fast runner
Paper ripper
Floppy ears
Soft belly
Black fur
House destroyer
Hates adults
Pencil chewer
Best pet in the world.

Tony Hamilton (9)
Kennoway Primary & Community School, Kennoway

Kennings – My Dog

Ball chaser
Colour brown
Loud barker
Excited jumper
Short walker
Dog bed
Garden runner
Snoozy snorer
Floppy ears
Tail wagger.

Cameron Manson (9)
Kennoway Primary & Community School, Kennoway

Rabbit – Kennings

Carrot cruncher
Cage nibbler
Vegetable chewer
Bunny jumper
Nose twitcher
Straw eater
Ear flopper
Little smiler
Best friend
Good pet.

Jade Smith (9)
Kennoway Primary & Community School, Kennoway

My Bulldog, Bella – Kennings

Stump wagger
Food begger
Fence jumper
Fast eater
Squishy face
Big ears
Really cute
Loud snorer
Cat chaser.

Mark Black (9)

Kennoway Primary & Community School, Kennoway

My Dog

Really cuddly
Cat hater
Very funny
Chicken lover
Bath disliker
Bone eater
Bed chewer
But a good friend.

Britney Payne (9)

Kennoway Primary & Community School, Kennoway

Penguin

P eckish for fish
E xcited to eat
N ever stops eating
G ets lots of fish
U nhappy if they don't get a fish
I n the sea they go and hunt
N ever live somewhere warm.

Lewis Doig (9)

Kennoway Primary & Community School, Kennoway

Rabbits

R abbits have lots of babies
A nd they can have rabies
B ut they don't eat meat
B ecause they are veggies
I nstead they like their greens
T hey come in different colours
S ometimes not like their mothers.

Declan Whyte (9)

Kennoway Primary & Community School, Kennoway

Wanted

W hen I'm sleeping I'm wanted
A nd every second I'm wanted
N ever time to myself
T oday and every day I'm wanted
E verybody shouts at me
D on't arrest me, please!

Dillan MacPhee (9)

Kennoway Primary & Community School, Kennoway

Happy

H appy times at Christmas
A lways get what I ask for
P lay with my Christmas toys
P lenty of things to do
Y ou can play with my toys.

Steven Todd (9)

Kennoway Primary & Community School, Kennoway

Dragon — Haiku

A four-legged beast
Breathes fire like no one else
He shall eat you now.

Ben Loughrey (10)

Kennoway Primary & Community School, Kennoway

Music Acrostic

M usic is peaceful
U nbearable music is terrible
S ounds lovely when you listen
I ncredible notes are bold
C rying to sad music.

Sam Paterson (9)

Kennoway Primary & Community School, Kennoway

My Dad Peter — Cinquain

His car
My dad is nice
We go to the bowling
He makes me happy when he drives
It's great!

Dylan Christie (10)

Kennoway Primary & Community School, Kennoway

Money Acrostic

M ake lots of money by working
O r save it all up
N ot to spend on junk
E nd of your money is not nice
Y ou don't have to spend it all in one day.

Jennifer Walker (9)

Kennoway Primary & Community School, Kennoway

Puppies – Cinquain

Puppies
They are little
Often they wag their tails
They like to go outside and play
So cute.

Ronnie Allison (9)

Kennoway Primary & Community School, Kennoway

Dragon – Cinquain

Dragon
Fire creatures
Red-hot, dangerous flames
Scorching, burning, blistering skin
Frighten.

Jordan McIntosh (9)

Kennoway Primary & Community School, Kennoway

Games Acrostic

G ames are good
A nd I have lots of them
M onopoly is my best board game
E veryone I play with has games
S miles when I win.

Lee Walker (9)

Kennoway Primary & Community School, Kennoway

Cosy Cottage

The frosted footsteps,
The red robin sings,
The white window,
The snow's white wings.

Chittering children,
Glittering trees,
Roasted marshmallows,
Delicate breeze.

Blue, grey and white,
I see all around,
Laughter and shouting,
That's the sound.

The snow is as white as a fluffy cloud,
The lake is a mirror on the frozen ground,
The mist is as soft as a feather,
As it twirls to the ground round and round.

Murrin Wallace (11)
Kincaidston Primary School, Ayr

People – Cinquain

People
Lovely, ugly
Talking, loving, hating
Playing and laughing together
Children.

Shaun Roberts (11)
Kincaidston Primary School, Ayr

The Blistering Blizzard

The blistering blizzard,
Was burning us up inside,
All the ponds
Turned into ice.

All the snowflakes,
Like a shining star,
All the mud,
Turned into tar.

Oh, the rain,
Spitting on my hand,
Oh, the rain,
It covers the whole land.

The whiteness of snow,
The trees are bare,
Everyone's freezing,
It just isn't fair.

Connor Rankin (11)
Kincaidston Primary School, Ayr

Dancing – Cinquain

Dancing
Hardcore so cool
Jumping, flipping, shouting
Hip hop, techno, gentle ballet
Party.

Jonathon McGugan (11)
Kincaidston Primary School, Ayr

My Wonderful Winter

As the snowflakes
Starts to dance in the breeze
Night falls and the
Lake begins to freeze.

As the birds sit
Chittering in the thorn
They watch as the
Day moves on.

As winter moves on
The snow is nearly gone
Spring is nearby
So let's keep a close eye.

Chloe Glass (11)
Kincaidston Primary School, Ayr

Cats – Kennings

Couch scratcher
Fish eater
Hair leaver
Bird killer
Noise maker
Self cleaner
Tree climber
Lap layer.

Emma Thomson (11)
Kincaidston Primary School, Ayr

Asylum – Kennings

Crazy place
Causing havoc
Mad looking
Bad looking
Breathtaking
Hair raising
Smells bad
Pitch black.

Zac Vallance (11)

Kincaidston Primary School, Ayr

Stick Insect – Kennings

Egg layer
Can't fly
Brave climber
Leaf muncher
Six legs
Skinny stick
Funny character.

John Gribbin (11)

Kincaidston Primary School, Ayr

Pancakes

Tasty treat
Flat, round
Syrup pouring
Frying sound
Flour, milk
Cracked eggs
Piled high.

Lisa McConnell (11)
Kincaidston Primary School, Ayr

Gerbils – Cinquain

Gerbils
Cuddly, cute, sweet
Playing, eating, sleeping
Nibbling stuff they're not supposed to
Rodent.

Hayley Scott (11)
Kincaidston Primary School, Ayr

Out In The Middle Of The Jungle

Out in the middle of the jungle,
Where the trees are big and tall,
Snakes roam out of their home,
Looking for food without being rude.
The bears are scary,
And very, very hairy,
Out in the middle of the jungle.

The plants are funny,
Some look like the colour of honey.
The bees come out the trees,
The soft, silky breeze,
Comes in and out the trees,
Out in the middle of the jungle.

The sun is always high,
In the light blue sky,
Out comes a mouse,
Running out of its house,
Now all the animals are here,
But none drinking beer,
Out in the middle of the jungle.

A tiger comes,
Holding something's lungs,
A little bird,
Is acting like a nerd,
It's very happy,
It's got a nappy,
Out in the middle of the jungle.

There's a big, bad lion,
Called Ryan,
A slimy snail,
Has found a nail,
Out in the middle of the jungle.

Darcey Bird (9)
Kirkmichael Primary School, Kirkmichael

Out In The Jungle

Out in the jungle,
Where nobody goes,
There's a big, fat lion,
Trying to eat your toes.

Out in the jungle,
Where nobody goes,
There's a big, brown bear,
Coming to eat your nose.

Out in the jungle,
Where nobody goes,
There's a big bee,
Coming to sting your toes.
Roar, grrr, buzz!

Ellie Blane (8)
Kirkmichael Primary School, Kirkmichael

At The Sea

One day I went to the sea,
I had good fun with Toby.
I saw seagulls, shells and crabs,
But there weren't any kebabs.
I could smell salt and seaweed,
And I really needed a feed,
So I had yummy sandwiches and a sweet,
I had to go home because I had sand on my feet.

Chloe Hodge (7)
Kirkmichael Primary School, Kirkmichael

The Milking

Cows eating silage,
Cows lying down,
Cows standing patiently,
Waiting to be milked.

Machine working quietly,
Milk flowing through the pipes,
Dad working the units,
Papa pressing buttons.

Cows walking to the shed,
Cows mooing softly,
Cows chewing the cud,
Waiting for morning.

Lewis Limond (9)
Kirkmichael Primary School, Kirkmichael

The Stray Rabbit

There is a stray rabbit,
He lives in the town,
His ears are floppy and brown.
He looks like a pompom with a frown,
He likes to sleep with a dressing gown,
But wakes in the middle of the night
And looks in the cupboard to get a fright!

Nikki Carter (8)
Kirkmichael Primary School, Kirkmichael

Puppy

P uppies are cute
U sually very sleepy
P uppies are different colours
P uppies like to jump
Y ou need a trained puppy.

Nicola Thom (10)
Kirkmichael Primary School, Kirkmichael

Bees

B usy, busy bees fast as can be
E asy to see, but sting my knee
E ven when I need a wee
S ting me when I eat my tea.

Cara Mundell (8)
Kirkmichael Primary School, Kirkmichael

Earth

E veryone should do their bit
A fter all it is our home
R euse, recycle, reduce
T his is the way to save the planet
H elp us to help the Earth.

Ross Mackay (8)
Murrayfield Primary School, Blackburn

The Door

(Inspired by 'The Door' by Miroslav Holub)

Go and open the door,
    Maybe outside there's a school
    Or a blue sky,
    Or a silly, dancing beagle.

Go and open the door,
    Maybe you'll see a snowman dancing,
    Maybe Jack Frost is frozen,
    Or silvery-white snow is falling.

Go and open the door,
    Even if it's only a bus coming your way,
    Even if there's only a lamp flickering,
    Even if there's only a policeman there,
    Go and open the door.

Even if nothing is there,
    Go and open the door.

        At least there is not a
        Dirty dog shaking his fur.

Rachel Murray (9)
New Cumnock Primary School, New Cumnock

The Door

(Inspired by 'The Door' by Miroslav Holub)

Go and open the door,
    Maybe outside there's a snowman,
    Or an igloo,
    Or a baby covered in ice.

Go and open the door,
    Maybe you'll see a shark singing,
    Or a running whale,
    Or a dolphin slapping itself.

Go and open the door,
    Even if there's only a dancing polar bear,
    Even if there's only a skipping leprechaun,
    Even if there's nothing there,
    Go and open the door.

Go and open the door,
    At least there's not a toast ghost.

Leiah Watson (9)

New Cumnock Primary School, New Cumnock

My Photo Album

That's me
Clapping my cats
They're asleep
On their mats

That's my sister
Smiling hard
Got a blister
On her hand

That's my mum
Long brown hair
Standing straight
Very rare

That's my dad
Making a face
Don't know why
What a disgrace!

Ceri Condie (9)

New Cumnock Primary School, New Cumnock

My Photo Album

That's me
I am one year old
Lying in my bed
Waiting to get fed

Here's my mum
Going to her wedding
To meet her husband
At the church

Here's my dad
Drunk on his birthday
Lost his shoe
He got a new Subaru

That's me and my mum
I was only 3 years old
Spaghetti everywhere
She was really mad!

Samantha Eakin

New Cumnock Primary School, New Cumnock

My Photo Album

That's me
Eating my birthday cake
My mum told me not to
Because I had a tummy ache.

Here's Gran
Sitting down
I ask her to play
With my toy clown.

Here's Dad
That day he had on a hat
I asked him
'Can we get a cat?'

Thomas Donnelly (9)
New Cumnock Primary School, New Cumnock

My Photo Album

That's me
Last month at Lochside
Wearing my favourite dress
Just going to get fresh air outside.

Here's my dad
With messy hair
Doing his best smiling
Standing on the stair.

There's my mum
She's got gorgeous nails
Got a purple dress on
With beautiful hair.

Alice Donaldson (9)

New Cumnock Primary School, New Cumnock

Creak, Creak!

Creak! Creak! The door flew open.
Bang! Bang! The window banged shut.
Tick-tock! Only a few minutes till 12 o'clock.
Ting-ting! The clock struck 12.
Howl! Howl! The wind went.
Rattle! Rattle! The leaves outside flew around.
Drip-drop! Went the downstairs tap.

Creak! Creak! Bang! Bang! Tick-tock! Ting-ting!
Howl! Howl! Rattle! Rattle! Drip-drop!
It's 5 o'clock.

Cairn Flaherty (9)

Ochiltree Primary School, Cumnock

What Has Happened To Michael

(Inspired by 'What Has Happened to Lulu?' by Charles Causley)

What has happened to Michael?
What has happened to Mike?
Last time I saw him he was running next to my bike,
That was the last time I saw Mike.

He was the best dog ever,
Even though he had fleas,
And every night at dinner time,
He'd finish my leftover peas.

My parents have tried to cheer me up,
By buying me a new bike,
But I'm still waiting for my answer,
What has happened to Mike?

John Brown (10)
Ochiltree Primary School, Cumnock

The Night Of Sounds

Bang! The old door bangs shut
Snap! A big branch from the tree snaps
Creak! The small window is blowing in the wind
Tick-tock! The big, wooden clock goes tick-tock
Pitter-patter! The rain goes pitter-patter on the big bay window
Squeak! The big, wooden door squeaks when it shuts
Clatter! Go the roof tiles when they fall off the roof
Drip-drop! The black drainpipe leaks.

Lyndsay Montgomerie (9)
Ochiltree Primary School, Cumnock

What Has Happened To Cheapy?

(Inspired by 'What Has Happened To Lulu?' by Charles Causley)

What has happened to Cheapy, Brother?
What has happened to Cheap?
His treats have not a bite,
Please! Help my parakeet . . .

Where has Cheapy gone to, Brother?
His cheep is sweet and fair.
I've searched up to the heavens,
Down the street. I hope he's not scared . . .

Why has he disappeared?
The window is wide open with toots.
The curtains are flying up and down.
Where is Cheapy? Oh, there he is, in my boots!

Lisa Parker (10)

Ochiltree Primary School, Cumnock

The Loud Night

Clatter! The trees fall down.
Ding-dong! Goes my doorbell.
Drip-drop! The downstairs tap is still on.
Creak! The wooden floorboards creak.
Splish-splash! The rain falls down.
Squeak! Go the mice under the floorboards.
Crack! The floorboards snap.
Tick-tock! Goes the grandfather clock.

Leah Goudie (9)

Ochiltree Primary School, Cumnock

Penguin

Mine is the squeak
That fills the air
From the beak
It is very rare.

Mine are the wings
That wish they could fly
To all places
I wonder why.

Mine are the eyes
That glow and stare
Do not look
Don't you dare.

Lewis Kahler (10)
Ochiltree Primary School, Cumnock

Night Of Sound

Tick-tock! Went the old loom.
Boom! Goes the loud thunder.
Snap! The balcony falls down!
Bang! The old door bangs shut!
Kablamo! Goes the hot microwave.
Smash! Goes the best vase.
Crash! The house falls down.

Jack Schendel (9)
Ochiltree Primary School, Cumnock

Horse

Mine is the heart breaking
When you hear a dog woof
The spotlight right on me
Me and my bleeding hoof

Mine is the eye
My back bleeds with the whip
I blind myself by looking up high
My foot is sore - I trip

Mine is the trot
Which I used to enjoy
Out in the field
Just me and my boy.

Karen Howat (10)
Ochiltree Primary School, Cumnock

Winter

W inter is very magical
I t is wonderful when it snows
N ever think there is nothing to do because there is lots
T he weather can be rough sometimes
E veryone is curled up next to the fire to keep warm
R eally dark in the morning and at night.

Morag Maguire (10)
Ochiltree Primary School, Cumnock

Polar Bear

Mine is the growl
That fills the air
The huntsmen follow it
They don't care.

Mine are the claws
Used to catch my prey
Wandering free
Each and every day.

Mine is the cream fur
The hunters want to trade
My fate is sealed
I am afraid.

Ryan Hutchison (10)
Ochiltree Primary School, Cumnock

Sound Poem

Bang! went the thunder and lightning.
Drip-drop! Went the heavy rain.
Ding-dong! Went the old doorbell.
Tick-tock! Went the new clock.
Splash! Went the river hitting the rock.

Josh Collins (9)
Ochiltree Primary School, Cumnock

Bear

Mine is the growl
In anger and despair
The circus caged me up
Does anyone care?

Mine is the face
That's laughed at in the ring
The screaming and the laughter
The circus leader believes he's a king.

Mine is the body
That jumps through fire
I'm scared and I'm shaking
They cut me with wire.

Rebecca Smeeton (10)
Ochiltree Primary School, Cumnock

Sounds In The Night!

Bang! the door slammed shut!
Creak! the old stairs fell down on top of a mouse.
Kaboom! the microwave blows up.
Smash! the window goes smash.

Eoghan Goudie (9)
Ochiltree Primary School, Cumnock

Bird

Mine are the wings
That flew in the sky
Up really high
But now I don't
I wonder why?

Mine were the eyes
That were very dark
But now I'm in a park.

Mine are the wings
That now droop low
They're now tied on a rope
That were once on show.

Aileen Harvey (10)
Ochiltree Primary School, Cumnock

Elephant

Mine is the trunk
The trumpet that fills the air
Grey is dull
It's not fair

Mine are the tusks
That have lost their shine
I'm so sad
All of the time

Mine are the eyes
I want to be free
I am hungry
So help me.

Tom Howat (10)
Ochiltree Primary School, Cumnock

A Night Of Sounds

Slam! The rusty front door slammed shut.
Tick-tock! The dusty old clock in the hall went tick-tock.
Splash! The rain outside went splash through the drainpipes.
Crack! The balcony on the side of the house went crack as it
                                                fell off.
Bang! The windows went bang as the wind swooshed through them.
Drip-drop! The rain drip-dropped as it hit the windows.
Crash! The flowerpots crashed as they fell from the dirty, narrow
                                           window ledge.
Squeak! The mice in the attic squeaked!
Ding-dong! The tree pushed against the doorbell, making it go
                                           ding-dong.

Amy Gatherer (9)
Ochiltree Primary School, Cumnock

Lost!

I see that he is lost.
He looks for his mum,
Who shouts, 'Come.'
He looks very sad,
But he might just add,
A yell or a scream,
In beside the cream.
His mum shouts,
'I'm beside the sweets,'
So he chances his luck
And asks for a couple of treats.
I hope that never happens to me.

Marc Perry (11)
St Aloysius' College, Glasgow

Lost!

I'll go to the shops
And buy some of Willie Wonka's famous Chocolate Pops.

I may have not had my dinner
And if I eat chocolate I'll be a big sinner.

My name is jack
And I want to have a six-pack.
I probably won't have that
Because of all the chocolate I eat, I'm bound to be fat.

I'm going to walk out of the door
And go to the shops and get some more.

I open my chocolate and there it is,
A golden ticket.
I wonder what you have to do with it.

It had some writing saying to come to my famous chocolate factory,
I couldn't wait.

I'm going to tell all of my mates,
I am the lucky boy,
Oh yes, this is so much better than a toy.

I go to the factory to get my chocolate,
I am jumping up and down and my mum tells me to stop it.

I go into the factory with the seven other kids,
Chocolate milk catches my eye
And it has a shiny lid.

I am so distracted,
When I go to ask Mr Wonka a question,
They have gone.

I don't really care,
For there is chocolate everywhere.
After a few moments I start to worry,
I hope they hurry, hurry, hurry!

My face is covered in chocolate sauce,
For I am lost.

Nicholas Querns (11)
St Aloysius' College, Glasgow

A Boy's Normal Day – The Drive Home From School

'So dear, what did you do at school today?'

'Oh, the usual. Jenkins took my ball again today
And threw it over the fence.
I forgot my PE kit again today
And ended up sitting on the bench.
You didn't pack my lunch again today,
I only had enough money for a pear
And I got a detention again today,
Because the teacher heard me swear.
I confessed my love to Isabelle again today,
She said she would not return that love, ever.
Claire got a gold star again today,
Because she thinks she's clever
And I know you always listen to Sis,
You never listen to me.'

'That's nice, dear,
But I was actually talking to you, Jayni.'

Niamh Kennedy (11)
St Aloysius' College, Glasgow

Lost!

Getting lost is a strange thing
Most people think it's not good
But it can be funny
And get you into the right mood.

There are many ways of getting lost
What jumps to mind are the woods
You could get lost in your house
Or from running away from people in hoods.

Some people get lost in strange ways
Like getting lost in a shop
My brother got lost in the oven
He looked like he was going to go pop!

But the worst way of getting lost
Is the way I'm about to show you
It doesn't involve slimy things
Or monsters that shout and go boo!

Getting lost in your mind
Is the worst over all
It's worse than getting lost in the countryside
Or getting lost in your hall.

You could end up in hairy fairyland
They might make you their queen
Or they could turn on you
Faster than you've ever seen.

You could end up in LaLa Land
With Po and Dipsy too
You might try and run away
But they're much faster than you

You see now how dangerous
The human mind can be
So you might want to stop daydreaming
Or you'll lose yourself, you'll see!

Elizabeth Carmichael
St Aloysius' College, Glasgow

Lost

Me and my mum in the supermarket,
Looking at the food,
Some looked so good I would steal it
If I could.

Mum was looking at the pasta,
I saw something big.
I went over to it,
It was a big, stuffed toy pig.

Then I realised I might get lost,
I thought, 'This isn't good.'
When I went back to Mum,
She had left the food.

Don't panic, I said to myself.
I checked all the aisles,
I couldn't find her anywhere,
So I started to make some calls.

I tried Dad and Gran,
It was a waste of money.
I looked beside the pig,
But it was just a big, stuffed bunny.

Then I saw Mum,
She shouted, 'Come!'
I dropped the mug
And gave her a big hug.

Seamus McGovern (11)
St Aloysius' College, Glasgow

In A Haunted House

As I entered the haunted house
By the light of the full moon
I could hear a creak
Then I found to my surprise
A werewolf was asleep.
Tiptoeing down the stairs
Right down to the coal-black cellar
Blood on the walls
Ghosts and ghouls everywhere
Not having much of a care.
Don't make a noise or they will hear and come over
Watch out, watch out, there are graves about
Here lies Murphy, the man with no hair
Unfortunately he was killed by a grizzly bear.
Look out the window
See the ghost of a vixen chasing a rabbit
Then she turned round and off at full speed
For the rabbit had four arms and magical charms.
Watch out, watch out, there's monsters about
Ready to eat you up
Not thinking about throwing up.
Bang go the shutters
Boom go the doors
Scary it may all seem
But it's just a dream.

Myles Docherty (11)
St Aloysius' College, Glasgow

Rain Through The Seasons

In Scotland there is rain in every season,
Spring, summer, autumn and winter,
Let's ponder . . .

Spring rain patters on the window
Tapping gently, inviting me to play with it,
Calling me in an encouraging whisper.

Summer rain floats wearily to the ground,
Winding its way and slowly forming shallow puddles,
Splashing and spluttering at irregular intervals.

Autumn rain tumbles and hisses,
Rolling its way, thundering to the drains,
Somersaulting through the stubborn leaves.

Winter rain pounds incessantly throughout the day,
Like a low-beat, thunderous drum,
Grabbing everything in its path,
Greedily consuming and drowning the icy gravel below.

Rain can never go away and when it returns,
The pounding starts again.

Connor Bilsland (11)
St Aloysius' College, Glasgow

Lost!

He didn't lose anything physical,
He didn't lose a precious possession,
Only his mind, only his will to live.

He no longer had any care for the world,
No care for anybody he knew or ever would,
No care for himself, the world was over.

He was being bulled,
Nobody had any respect for him, if he couldn't pay it back.

Soon after, his teachers gave up on him,
He was a wreck, a hopeless little boy who didn't attempt to
make friends,
Or have any fun.

Failing tests and exams, he began to wonder,
What is life like on the other side?
What would happen if he left this world
And started again?

I have nothing left here,
I have nothing to lose.

Matthew McArthur (11)
St Aloysius' College, Glasgow

Gold!

Gold costs thousands of pounds
But you need equipment to go underground
To capture the gold and become filthy rich
Own your favourite football team and pitch
Be in magazines, roles in films and be a star
All because of a golden bar.

Makeshift gold-hunting material
Some of it was rusty so I used antibacterial
Metals like iron and dirty tins
Pick up gold into big dustbins
Making this was rather hard
It was worth it though because of the search for golden bars.

Found the perfect spot to find
Chunks of gold, shapes of all kinds
After a day of gold-less searching
My wonder machine suddenly stopped working
My super-stardom dream went
Me penniless, not a pound, euro or cent.

Helen Devine (11)
St Aloysius' College, Glasgow

Pollution

There is something that goes all over the world
But it has no legs or feet.
It's got no lungs, no hair or mouth
And our environment it eats.

There is an easy way to prevent it
And it really isn't a chore,
Just switch off a light and recycle your cans
And we'll live for evermore!

Everyone can help
In their own little way,
It's so easy to do,
You could save the day!

It really is a horrible crime,
When we say it's a load of rubbish,
But all the animals are dying,
So are the trees, bugs and fish.

Lucie Dunne (11)
St Aloysius' College, Glasgow

Lost

Twigs cracking underneath my feet
I can hardly see with all the sleet
With my arms cold and my feet almost freezing
I can't see any of it easing

Pine and oak are my only surroundings
I doesn't help with the thunder pounding.

Iain McKirdy (11)
St Aloysius' College, Glasgow

A Windy Day

One annoying day when the
Grass was wet as a wet shower,
The wind was bellowing like a banshee.

The wind was blowing with power,
Strong and muscular bodies pushing
Against your face with a lot
Of pace. Exhausts whistling full
Of petrol. A coat of frost on the trees.

Houses full of warming heat.
Always pale and red.
Lights are lit bright as a kite,
Warm and cosy the house is.

Garden full of silver frost,
Jack Frost's cost. Near the
Night, cold and dark. So that
Is what winter is.

John McIntyre (12)
St Aloysius' College, Glasgow

Lost!

I was at the shops with my bro,
Then suddenly, I saw a tennis pro!
I ran towards him, past a toy giraffe,
(I really wanted his autograph!)
I looked behind me to check if Joseph was there,
But for a tennis player, he didn't seem to care!
But there was a reason for Joseph not to like
A guy that turned out to be a look-alike!

Past shelves of food and ice-cold drinks
And endless aisles of fluffy pinks,
When wondering how much all this would cost,
I finally decided that I was lost.
I was about to panic and start to pout,
When I spotted him at the checkout.

I decided that I should never run off,
Not even if I was attacked by a Goth.

Matthew Travers (11)
St Aloysius' College, Glasgow

Lost!

I was walking my dog,
He ran into a forest chasing a frog.
I ran after him,
Shouting, 'Jim, Jim!'

The trees were so high,
If I fell off one, I would surely die.
I looked in the lake, I looked under logs,
But I just couldn't find my very bad dog.

I didn't know where I was,
I came into a complete pause!
I started to panic,
It was just tragic!

I was running, trying to find a way out,
When I came across a bear at the lake,
Trying to catch a very big trout!

Emma Eusebi (11)
St Aloysius' College, Glasgow

Lost!

Help! No! Oh dear!
I'm lost in another dimension and now I'm stranded here!
There are fire-breathing horses with great, red, rolling eyes
And flying sheep who can speak! One said to me, 'Oh hi!'

Help! No! Oh dear!
I fell into an enchanted pool and now I'm a flying deer!
I'm truly stranded here!

Niamh Campbell (11)
St Aloysius' College, Glasgow

Stinky Milinky

He stomped over vegetable patches,
He bumped into doors,
He sniffed at his bottom
And scratched all the floors.
What would he do next?
Well, that Stinky Milinky
Caused, oh so much grief,
He was an absolute thief!

Stinky Milinky,
Was dafter than daft,
A silly and adventurous,
Stupid cat.
He had bruises on his tail
And a very loud wail, oh,
The noise of his wail!

Hannah Stubbs (11)
St Aloysius' College, Glasgow

I Am A Tree

When I hear the wind rustle in my ear
And the leaves sprinting past my fingers
I feel that I am the king of height

I can see the birds looking into my eyes
And the squirrels running around my feet
The sound of my arms flapping around from the wind
And the foxes howling in the night
I feel like I am the master of might.

Charlie Lonergan (11)
St Aloysius' College, Glasgow

What If . . .

(Inspired by 'What If?' by Shel Silverstein)

Last night, while I lay thinking here,
Some Whatifs crawled inside my ear
And pranced and partied all night long
And sand their same old Whatif song:
Whatif I don't get a girlfriend?
Whatif the sky falls on top of me?
Whatif my parents get broke?
Whatif I get run over?
Whatif I lose my arms?
Whatif I'm in a plane that crashes?
Whatif I become as flat as a pancake?
Whatif I get pulled out to sea?
Everything seems swell, and then
The nightmare Whatifs strike again.

Douglas Lockhart (11)
St Aloysius' College, Glasgow

Last Day At School

When it turns nine o'clock, I will line up one last time,
Because at the end of the day I'll be history
And it's time for me to leave.

I went to class with all my friends,
And they kindly gave me some gifts.

Coming to lunch I ate some grub,
Then I went outside to play football.
Later that day the bell rang to say,
That I'm nearly history because it's nearly one o'clock.

It turns three o'clock, I go outside,
A tear drops from my eye,
My friends start to cry,
I told them, 'Farewell my friends,
This is the end but I'll keep in touch.'

Michael Eusebi (11)

St Aloysius' College, Glasgow

Lost

'My handbag!' shouted Mum.
'Pull up the car, right now! Ta!'
I had never seen Mum in so much hysteria,
So much that she could blow up the whole play area.
She was shouting, screaming, having a fit,
I just wanted to be in the desert digging a pit!

We rushed to the café to see if the bag was there,
By the time we arrived, it was all by itself and covered in hair.
Mum was happy, but puzzled as well,
Why was her bag covered in hair?

The owner of the café didn't really care,
So we threw in a big brown bear
To munch his newly groomed hair!

Mariateresa Cascio (11)
St Aloysius' College, Glasgow

The Shipwreck

I lie here at the bottom of the sea,
Rotting away every few minutes.

I used to soar across the Atlantic,
But then I hit the iceberg . . .

I have many valuables lying around me,
My bow has almost disappeared.

Within a few years I will be gone,
I am the Titanic,
And I am fading away.

Mairead Corrigan (11)
St Aloysius' College, Glasgow

Royal Stew

I'm thinking of stewing the queen,
It will be such a wonderful scene,
With jewels and diamonds
And fur and felt,
Only to serve it to me!

I'm thinking of stewing the queen,
But how?
But when?
But where?
I'll add lots of ingredients, like carrots, peas,
Maybe beans, I don't know,
My ideas just grow,
That's how I'll stew the queen!

Emma Canning
St Aloysius' College, Glasgow

What If . . .

(Inspired by 'Whatif' by Shel Silverstein)

As I lay in bed, some whatifs crawled into my ear
And this is what they sounded like:

Whatif my TV blows up?
Whatif my house gets crushed?
Whatif all my gadgets get set alight?
Whatif school did not exist?
But all these things are not real
Because they're all whatifs.

Finn Corrigan (11)
St Aloysius' College, Glasgow

The Last Day Of School

It was the last day of school
And I was feeling very happy
Until a bully pushed me down
He turned my smile into a frown

I told him that he was a bully
But he didn't seem to care
When I got up he took my money
His friends said he was funny

The final bell rang
It's time for a holiday
I had no choice but to run away
Then the bully shouted, 'I'll get you someday!'

Alasdair McConnell (11)
St Aloysius' College, Glasgow

In Trouble

I nnocent I am
N o proof you have

T errible boy I can be, but not
R ight now
O ut the window you say, I'm
U nable to land right
B last! I hit the ground
'L et me out,' I cry.
E ventually, I come up for another go.

Alessandro Capaldi (12)
St Aloysius' College, Glasgow

Last Day At School

Would anyone miss her when she had gone?
Would anyone phone and ask her to come along?

They won't want to see her when she has gone
The friends that she had
And that's not many at all

She ran down the lane, tears in her eyes
Got into the car and said, 'Mum, take me home'
As the car slowly drove away
She watched the others coming out of school
None of them looked upset
Only her, in the car on her own.

Hannah McLaughlin (11)
St Aloysius' College, Glasgow

Lost!

I was in Xscape with my dad you see
I was on the ski slope with him and me.

I was doing big 360 jumps
And an hour later I had the mumps.

We had lost my dad's credit cards,
So we asked the bodyguards.

If they had seen them on the ground,
'Cause they were worth more than 1,000 pounds.

In the end we found the cards,
And I thought oh, hey that wasn't so hard.

Jonathan Sweeney (11)
St Aloysius' College, Glasgow

The Last Gasp!

S tars drift by peacefully
P T3000 my rocket, floating in the sky
A ll the planets swirling and soaring all around me
C omets flash before my eyes
E ver such beautiful planets sparkle in the light of the moon

T reacherous sounds, the engine gives a bang
R oaring fires suddenly emerge!
A hh . . . there goes PT3000
V enus and Mars fly quickly past me
E very second closer to death
L ast gasp . . .

Theodora Hill (11)
St Columba's Primary School, Cupar

Deadly Objects

S treaming through the atmosphere
P reparing for touchdown
A ll the crew to action stations
C argo doors slam open
E mpty wasteland lies ahead

T he crew taking samples of Mars
R ight ahead moving objects pass
A ll the objects turn, making everyone's adrenalin pump rapidly
V ery weird life forms move to us
E veryone runs for his life
L anding craft is set for escape.

Paul Eddie (11)
St Columba's Primary School, Cupar

Space Travel

S pace shuttle engine thrusting up 3, 2, 1
P eople ecstatic as the space shuttle launches into space
A stonished as they enter extraordinary surroundings of space
C rammed environment
E xciting views they soon discover

T he incredible views become breathtaking
R emarkable planets and stars we pass
A steroid field we enter
V isiting space has been an extraordinary experience
E ntering the gravity field to Earth
L anding the spacecraft safely.

Adam Breckons (11)

St Columba's Primary School, Cupar

Space Travel

S ophisticated high tech machinery to take us to space
P lanets surrounding us wherever we go
A stronauts going round searching for life on other planets
C laustrophobic, cramped rocket
E ventually we land

T aking samples for scientists to test
R eckless rockets left behind
A liens spying on us - will they attack?
V isiting Venus, volcanoes erupting
E vermore I won't forget this moment
L ost forever.

Naomi Pereira (11)

St Columba's Primary School, Cupar

Remembrance Day

R unning soldiers fighting for their lives
E ntering bloody battlefields, weapons at the ready
M aking their mark on worldwide history
E very day brings more grief, but one step closer to victory
M arking the lives of all the fighters brings honour to them all
B oys' limbs flying aimlessly
R ed poppies marking fatal risks
A s deaths become as common as air
N o pride was lost
C rying, mourning, waiting at home
E ach a hero of the world.

Abigail Cumming (11)
St Columba's Primary School, Cupar

No One To Hold

S tranded on an island of sadness and horror
H eartbroken Shmuel longing to see his family
M ortified, not knowing what's going on
U nknowing that death is on its way
E ndeavouring to start his life again
L ifeless with no one to hold.

Amy Wilson (11)
St Columba's Primary School, Cupar

What A Bad Life!

S itting horrified on an island of torture
H orrendous soldiers beating him by the minute
M isery creeping up on him
U nlucky, poor little boy, Shmuel in a concentration camp
E ndless death
L eads to a torture in Hell!

Sadie Colley (11)
St Columba's Primary School, Cupar

Homecoming

Oh, long ache in my bones
And the fear in my head.
Suffering and guts in my heart
Makes me dread belting up in armour.
I can't move.
My slow steed is suffering too.
It's damp and dark and dreadful
Shut like steel to the sun
In the war.

Sun shining in my face
I am there!
I am home!
No ache in my bones
No fear in my head
No suffering and guts in my heart
I am home.

Sophie Innes (9)
St Leonard's School, St Andrews

Wings

If I had wings
I would touch the sun
Until my nails glowed with pleasure

If I had wings
I would smell the burnt rock
From the moon

If I had wings
I would taste the sticky stars

If I had wings
I would see the mighty God
Upon the Earth

If I had wings
I would hear the wild wind
Blow the crazy clouds further and further away!

Abby Hay (8)
St Leonard's School, St Andrews

Sea Horses And Eels – Haikus

Sea horses
Magical creatures
Two sea horses under sea
Playing foolishly.

Eels
Gliding through the sea
Making ripples underneath
The sea is wriggling.

Inés Hayward–Daventry
St Leonard's School, St Andrews

If I Had Wings

If I had wings,
I would touch the moon with my own two hands like never before.

If I had wings,
I would taste a chunk of cloud and think of candyfloss.

If I had wings,
I would hear the people shouting and screaming to each other.

If I had wings,
I would look down at the mountains and see how tall they
                                              really are.

If I had wings,
I would sniff the sun to see if it smelt like pepper.

If I had wings,
I would use them very carefully.

Catriona Cleary (8)
St Leonard's School, St Andrews

My Bedroom

I love my bedroom
It's the best place to be!
It's warm
It's cosy
But it's messy.
My teddy is knitted by my gran
Mum is always telling me to tidy up, but I don't care.
My big, woollen cosy made by Mum
And the blanket made by Dad.

Rachel Hamilton (9)
St Leonard's School, St Andrews

The Train Driver

Don't let him drive the train,
He's mad,
He's bad.
Don't let him drive the train,
He'll make us swim,
Or make the train dim.
Don't let him drive the train,
He'll put glue on our seats,
Then make us dead meat.
Don't let him drive the train,
He'll eat us alive,
Then put us in a big, fat pie.
Don't let him drive the train . . .
'For goodness sake, Tim, tidy your room
and stop playing!'

Ljubica Damjanovic (9)
St Leonard's School, St Andrews

Mummy

If she was water, she would be smooth like a lake
If she was a bird, a friendly robin
If she was an animal, she would be a gentle guinea pig
On Saturdays and Sundays she hugs me
Cuddling up in bed
Mum with smooth brown hair
Dancing in the sun
Mummy's voice slipping in my ear
Flowery smelling Mum.

James Gray (8)
St Leonard's School, St Andrews

Homecoming

The knight is coming home
Helmet shiny in the sun
Strong as steel
He thought he was going to die
But his crusade is over.

The portcullis is down
The door is huge in front of him
This damp, dark door is shut tight
He knocks on the door
In he goes

It is as dark as night in the castle
But greeted by his dog
He's happy to be home.

Jake Braun (8)
St Leonard's School, St Andrews

Sandcastle

S mooth sand
A big wave coming in
N ot a cloud to be seen
D olphins playing in the sea
C rabs scuttling side to side
A ship setting off to Germany
S hips racing to Mexico
T all flags waving around
L ittle by little my sandcastle goes
E verything's gone off my sandcastle.

Katherine McBarron (9)
St Leonard's School, St Andrews

Summer's Cloud

S ummer's day, flying away in an aeroplane
U zbekistan is where we're going today
M ummy says we're away for a month
M mm, their food is lovely
E ven though my brother is being really annoying, it is still
    the best
R eally one day gone
S eals are far away

C louds are up, up in the sky
L ovely summer's day
O h wow, the beach is lovely
U seful to have a bucket and spade
D addy says this is the end and time to go home.

Aeonie Ramsay (9)
St Leonard's School, St Andrews

Bye—Bye House

Oh house, all those years,
So many cheers.
All those days,
Listen to those hoorays.
Wonder what it will be like?
Where will I put my bike?
Now we are all out of town,
Oh no, I forgot to pack my dressing gown.
Bye-bye friendly home,
Now I hear the car's boring drone.

Caitlin Donald (9)
St Leonard's School, St Andrews

If I Had Wings

If I had wings
I would fly to the moon
And see the stars sparkle.

If I had wings
I would dance on lily pads
And smell the lily's sweet smell.

If I had wings
I would hear the birds in the air
Singing on and on.

If I had wings
I would taste the sweet taste
Of brambles.

Amber Edmiston (8)
St Leonard's School, St Andrews

Here We Go Again!

Here we go again,
Down the street, over the hill.

Here we go again,
In the soggy, wet car.

Here we go again,
Down to the crunchy beach.

But Mum!

Olivia Bourne (9)
St Leonard's School, St Andrews

The Fair Is Coming

The fair is coming,
Let's shout and cheer,
The fair is coming,
It's here, it's here!

There is candyfloss and hot dogs
And a magician who turns people into frogs,
But the fair is here,
Yippee, yippee!

It is time to go home,
Oh no, oh no!
I don't want to be alone,
So I am never going to go.

Emma Stevenson (9)
St Leonard's School, St Andrews

Ten Things Found In A Climber's Pocket

(Inspired by '10 Things Found In A Wizard's Pocket' by Ian McMillan)

A piece of chalk in a chalk bag.
A dried up worm.
Signed copy of Roald Dahl's 'The Enormous Crocodile'.
A broken compass with a spinning needle.
A pencil sharpener with no blade.
A broken rope about 5cm long.
Karabiners.
A packet of Chewits.
A Swiss Army knife, but rusting.
A Lego man with no legs.

Mats Cole (9)
St Leonard's School, St Andrews

If I Had Wings

If I had wings
I would go to the Bermuda Triangle
I think it would be long like a tunnel

To touch

If I had wings
I would hear the wind in the tunnel

If I had wings
It would smell like salt in the sea in the triangle

If I had wings
I would come back and put on the News at 10
But it won't happen.

Stuart Kirchacz (9)
St Leonard's School, St Andrews

Homecoming

'H ere he comes,' shout the guards.
O nwards he walks towards the bridge in his heavy chainmail.
M aking the worst clanking ever
E veryone trying to open the wooden door to the castle
C omes his wife and Harry the dog, acting as if he was a
    puppy again
O h so happy
M ighty rejoicing
I n all the land
N ow the townspeople come out
G ood feasting in the great hall.

Ellie Costa Sa (9)
St Leonard's School, St Andrews

Ten Things Found In A Policeman's Pocket

(Inspired by '10 Things Found In A Wizard's Pocket' by Ian McMillan)

Sweeties wrapped in shiny, coloured foil
A spare bullet - I wonder where that came from?
Bubblegum to keep him happy
A walkie-talkie still blaring crackly messages
A rusty knife with a broken blade
A bunch of assorted keys - 'home', 'car', 'cuffs'
A crisp, white hankie wrapped carefully round a
                    suspicious-looking weapon
A whistle on a thick, metal chain
A neat, pencil-shaped torch
A few loose pound coins.

Hamish Miles (9)
St Leonard's School, St Andrews

Original Owl

Courageous claws clashing
As it grips its prey
Cutting like a knife through cake
Bone-breaking beak
Almost like steel, as strong as silver rock
Eagle eye
The owl is a flying demon.

Jamie MacAulay (8)
St Leonard's School, St Andrews

Class

Kids talking
Teacher shouting
Kids go quiet
Teacher leaving
Kid goes crazy
Boy screams
Glue flying
Scissors breaking
Rulers snapping
Teacher is back
Shouting . . .
'Detention!'

Georgia Laird (10)
St Leonard's School, St Andrews

If I Had Wings

If I had wings I would taste the stars as sharp as knives,
I would sit on the clouds as soft as silk,
I would listen to the wind whispering its deepest secrets,
I would smell the sunset as colourful as a chameleon.

But most of all, if I had wings I would slide down the rainbow
To see if there really is a pot of gold at the end!

Maddie Anstruther (8)
St Leonard's School, St Andrews

In The Airport

In the airport there are people bustling around,
Some in the air and some on the ground.
Rushing, rushing, here and there,
I see people everywhere.
In the cafes, in the shops,
There are so many people here, I might pop.

Flora Adam (9)

St Leonard's School, St Andrews

If I Had Wings

If I had wings I would touch the sky
I would eat a lullaby
I would sunbathe in the sky
I would smell fresh air
I would hear my heart
I would sit on the sun.

Marina Drysdale (8)

St Leonard's School, St Andrews

If I Had Wings

If I had wings I would see the sun glow brightly
I would taste a cloud as soft as candyfloss
I would feel a star as sharp as a knife
I would smell fresh air in the sky
I would hear the wind howling
If I had wings I could do anything.

Sophie McMillan (8)
St Leonard's School, St Andrews

The Journey

We were walking down the lane
When we saw a plane
So we walked to the train
In the heavy rain
On the train we gambled
And money we did gain.

Colin Christie (9)
St Leonard's School, St Andrews

Garden — Haiku

Sunshine glimmering
Flowers growing happily
Children playing games.

Olivia Carslaw (10)
St Leonard's School, St Andrews

Egyptians

E gyptians believed firmly that with proper preparation
   a person could live again after death.
G ods were worshipped in temples.
Y oung Tutankhamun died at 18 years old.
P erfume, oils and resins were used on the body to make it soft.
T utankhamun's death mask was blue and yellow
   and was made of gold.
I sis was the god of motherhood.
A mun was the god of air and of Thebes. His name means hidden.
N atron salt was what they put onto the body
   to remove the water.
S phinx was half-man, half-lion and guarded the pyramids.

Olivia Black (8)
St Patrick's Primary School, Greenock

Egyptians

E gyptians were found by Howard Carter.

G ods were buried in pyramids, the Valley of the Queens
and Valley of the Kings.

Y ou can still go to see pharaohs' tombs in pyramids today.

P yramids were built from thousands of heavy stone blocks,
all cut by hand.

T ombs had all sorts of things in them, like food and slaves.

I sis was married to Osiris but they were also brother and sister.

A nubis is the god of mummifying and death.

N ile Delta went up to the Mediterranean Sea.

S phinx is a half-man, half-lion and it sits
in the middle of the desert!

Jemma Renfrew (8)

St Patrick's Primary School, Greenock

Egyptians

E very Egyptian pharaoh got mummified when they died.

G ods and goddesses the Egyptians worshipped.

Y ou would probably have been an Egyptian slave
if you were not rich.

P eople who died would have to pass the underworld tests
to get to the afterlife.

T he gobbler ate your heart if it weighed more
than the feather of truth.

I sis was the goddess of the Underworld.

A nubis was the god of mummification.

N atron salt they used to dry out the body.

S carab beetles the Egyptians worshipped.

Nicole McGhee (8)

St Patrick's Primary School, Greenock

Egyptians

E gypt is in the north of Africa.
G ods were worshipped in temples.
Y ou could be buried in pyramids.
P apyrus was the paper the Egyptians used.
T utankhamun became king when he was 8 years old
   and died when he was 19.
I sis was the god of motherhood.
A n asp bit Cleopatra.
N atron salt was poured over all the dead bodies
   to suck out all the water.
S eth was the god of chaos.

Rhianne O'Neill (8)
St Patrick's Primary School, Greenock

Egyptians

E gypt used to be divided into upper and lower Egypt.
G iant pyramids were built for pharaohs.
Y ou would have to carry lots and lots of gold to a king's tomb.
P apyrus was made out of reeds.
T he person who found Tutankhamun's tomb
   was named Howard Carter.
I sis was Osiris' wife.
A n Egyptian boy would have a single plait of hair
   on the right hand side of his head.
N atron salt was used when mummifying.
S phinx is an Egyptian monument.

Francesca Fisher (8)
St Patrick's Primary School, Greenock

Egyptians

E gyptians lived a long time ago.
G ods and goddesses were worshipped in Egypt.
Y ellow and blue were the colours of Tutankhamun's death mask.
P apyrus was the paper the Egyptians wrote their hieroglyphics on.
T utankhamun married one of his half-sisters.
I f you go to Egypt today you can see the tombs and pyramids.
A mulets were wrapped in the linen bandages
     when the pharaohs were mummified.
N atron salt was put over the body to dry up
     the water in the body.
S phinx was half-man, half-lion and protected the pyramids.

Megan Rodgers (8)
St Patrick's Primary School, Greenock

Egyptians

E gyptians believed that when they died
     they could go to the afterlife.
G ods were very powerful. Egyptians believed in them.
Y ears ago Tutankhamun lived.
P yramids were built to hold great tombs.
T utankhamun married his half-sister.
I nside the tombs were the treasures and mummies.
A khenaton was Tutankhamun's father.
N efertiti was Tutankhamun's stepmother.
S ometimes slaves got put in coffins alive.

Rian Montgomery (8)
St Patrick's Primary School, Greenock

Egyptians

E gyptians worshipped over 2000 gods and goddesses.
G ood Egyptians went to the afterlife.
Y ears and years the Egyptians lived for.
P yramids took over 20 years to build!
T utankhamun was very famous
    but he only ruled Egypt for 9 years.
I sis is the goddess of motherhood.
A mulets were put on mummies.
N efertiti was married to Akhenaton.
S pecial treasures were put in the tombs.

Joshua Ruddy (8)
St Patrick's Primary School, Greenock

Egyptians

E gypt is in North Africa where it is very hot,
    they had to work hard growing crops.
G ods and goddesses were worshipped by all of the Egyptians.
Y ears ago the Egyptians lived.
P haraohs had to be buried in pyramids.
T utankhamun was the youngest pharaoh.
I sis was married to Osiris who was the god of the Underworld.
A n asp bit Cleopatra when she was pharaoh.
N atron salt was used when mummifying the dead bodies.
S ome animals were worshipped just like gods and goddesses.

Eilis McDowell (8)
St Patrick's Primary School, Greenock

Egyptians

E gyptians were slaves to kings and queens.
G ods were very rich so were kings and queens.
Y ou might be a queen or king of Egypt.
P apyrus was a paper you wrote on and was made of reeds.
T utankhamun was the boy king.
I mhotep was a famous Egyptian architect.
A n Egyptologist is looking for the tombs of the pharaohs.
N ile Delta is where the River Nile
    runs into the Mediterranean Sea.
S eth is the god of chaos.

Chelsea Gault (8)
St Patrick's Primary School, Greenock

Egyptians

E gyptian slaves built big pyramids for their pharaohs.
'G et a move on slave!' said the pharaoh from up in his palace.
Y ou would probably not have wanted to be an Egyptian mummy!
P yramids are what the pharaohs were buried in.
T utankhamun was the young boy pharaoh,
    he died at 18 years old.
I sis was married to Osiris, her brother.
A nd the afterlife was a paradise for an Egyptian pharaoh.
N atron salt was used to take the water out of the mummy's body.
S obek is a god with a crocodile head.

Emily McColgan (8)
St Patrick's Primary School, Greenock

Egyptians

E gyptians believed that when you died you went to the afterlife.
G oods and all things precious went into the tombs.
Y ears ago there was a boy king called Tutankhamun.
P eople in Ancient Egypt had lots of gods.
T utankhamun was a most famous pharaoh.
I sis was the god of motherhood.
A nubis is the god of death.
N ile Delta is near the Mediterranean Sea.
S ome ancient Egyptians were rich but some were poor.

Anna Johnson (8)
St Patrick's Primary School, Greenock

Egyptians

E gyptians worshipped cats.
G raves of the Egyptians were called tombs.
Y ears ago Egyptians built giant pyramids.
P haraohs ruled over the Egyptians.
T utankhamun was the most famous Egyptian king.
I sis was the god of motherhood.
A ncient Egypt was a very sandy place.
N ile is the name of the great river in Egypt.
S ecrets were carved on the walls.

Ross Meechan (8)
St Patrick's Primary School, Greenock

Egyptians

E gypt is in North Africa where it is very hot.
G ood people went to the afterlife.
Y ears go by, but the pyramids still stood.
P erfumes and oil were put on the body when mummifying.
T he Egyptians worshipped over 1000 gods and goddesses.
I sis was married to Osiris and they were brother and sister.
A nubis was the god of mummification.
N atron salt was put on the body when mummifying.
S ome of the Egyptians were poor but most of them were rich.

Ellie Wilkie (8)
St Patrick's Primary School, Greenock

My Little Dinosaur

My little dinosaur is called Minmi
In the films he's black and white
The twigs and trees will quiver
Before he gets a bite
The T-rex will challenge him
To a big almighty fight
He says, 'I'm going to punch you
Sometime in the night!'

Lewis MacDougall (8)
St Patrick's Primary School, Greenock

My Stegosaurus

I have a stegosaurus.
He is rather sweet.
But he is very, very fussy
About the food that he will eat.
I offered him a hot dog but . . .
He looked at me and said,
'Are you a crazy girl?'
So I gave him a carrot instead.

Jana O'Donnell (8)
St Patrick's Primary School, Greenock

Tyrannosaurus Rex

T-rex was a king
What a thing
Eating, chewing my brother
And also my mother
Don't look in his eyes
Or he will make you fry.

Evan Stewart (9)
St Patrick's Primary School, Greenock

My Baby T-Rex

I had a baby T-rex
Nothing would he eat
'Maybe a baby child' he said,
'That will do,
I might have you!'

Caera Davis (8)
St Patrick's Primary School, Greenock

I Wish I Was A Dinosaur

I wish I was a dinosaur
I'd call myself Maurice,
I'd sleep beside my teddy all night
And I'd call my teddy, Horace.

Kay Lapsley (7)
St Patrick's Primary School, Greenock

My Ankylosaurus

I have an ankylosaurus
Who sleeps beside my bed
I love my ankylosaurus
Although I'd like a T-rex instead!

Jay King (7)
St Patrick's Primary School, Greenock

My T-Rex

My T-rex is the king
But when he starts to sing
People bring their earmuffs.

Jodi McMath (8)
St Patrick's Primary School, Greenock

Him

My foot crashes down into a puddle of water,
It's him -
The one who is making me run.
Thud! My bag hits my leg again.

It's not my fault,
Hussein is a common middle name where I come from.
'Oi, where ya going?'
He shouts this!
He slows down; I know what's coming.

Dead end, fear crawls all over me like a spider.
An evil smile slips onto his face,
His face is dark with hate,
His eyes are cold and empty.

Then I hear a footstep,
The evil smile on his face fades away.
I see who it is, it's the teacher,
He's heard and seen everything!
Now, I'm the one smiling . . .

I always smile now.

Jack Proudfoot (12)
St Peter's RC Primary School, Edinburgh

The New Girl

The new girl
always moving from house to house
that's what I was called.
As I went from school to school
shiny new school shoes
clean, crisp uniform.
I was like a bird
flying to new places,
but bullies were obstacles,
lurking round corners
waiting for their prey.

Phones;
they can take photos . . .
videos
send messages
any bully's key weapon.
I shrunk when photos and videos
got sent from phone to phone
rumours spread . . .
about me
they were jealous,
just jealous.

I had to face them at school
no one knew
how I was feeling,
the endless looks,
the endless murmurs:
when I passed in the corridors
I heard snippets of conversation
circling around me
about me.

One day: the confidence came
from . . . somewhere
the magic came to me

I answered them
ignored the photos
and texts the videos
and they got bored
because I didn't care.
They stopped
people became more friendly
the tears stopped trailing down my cheeks;
I was happy
and together
my friends and me
we stood up to the bullies
together . . .
the power of people.

Louise Goode (11)
St Peter's RC Primary School, Edinburgh

Why Was It Me?

Why was it me
That got left out of games?
That was picked on because of my height?

Why was it me
That everyone whispered about
And nobody ever talked to?

Why was it me
That had to have a different colour of skin
And came from a different country?

Why was it me
That felt
Smaller and smaller every second . . .

Theresa Wong (11)
St Peter's RC Primary School, Edinburgh

What's The Difference?

What's the difference,
Between you and me?
We both go to school,
Like everyone else I can see.
What's the difference,
Between you and me?
We both have a family,
And live by the sea.
What's the difference,
Between you and me?
We both have friends,
Yours is called Lee.
What's the difference,
Between you and me?
We both love animals,
All except bees.
What's the difference,
Between you and me?
We both love art,
And French and RE.
What's the difference,
Between you and me?
We both go to basketball lessons
And neither of us pay a fee.
What's the difference,
Between you and me?
I love to dance, unlike you
And when we do it in PE I jump with glee.
What's the difference,
Between you and me?
You pay for piano lessons,
I get them free.
Could that be it?
No.
What's the difference,
Between you and me?

You're good at the high jump,
Unlike me, I fell down and hurt my knee.
Could that be it?
No.
Ah!
Now I understand,
I'm black and you're not.
I wish people would stop being racist,
Now!

Deborah Nicol (11)
St Peter's RC Primary School, Edinburgh

Racism Is Wrong! Don't Do It!

I wish that racism would go and never come back.
It's not fair to make fun of people's skin colour
Whether it is brown, white or black.

I think racism is wrong and bad
It drives me crazy, it drives me mad.
I think racism isn't fair
And I would put people in jail for it if I was the mayor.
Some people think it's fun but that's because they don't care.

I want racism to stop
So that world would be tip-top.
People think racism is cool
And whoever thinks that, they are a mule.

Racism is cruel
And if you don't think that you are a fool.
I don't like the people that are racist
I think they are wrong and must be dealt with
Take a stand and show racism the red card!

Lucy Conway (10)
St Peter's RC Primary School, Edinburgh

Once I Was A Bully

I used to have friends,
I used to have a lot,
Well at least that's what I thought,
But the truth was, they were scared of me,
Scared of what I could be.

I enjoyed the bullying,
I liked being big and tough,
I liked being mean, I liked being rough,
I liked being mean and bad,
I liked making other people feel sad.

I enjoyed bullying,
I enjoyed bullying very much,
I bullied that kid who spoke Dutch,
I bullied those who were different or small,
I bullied those who wore glasses, those who were tall.

But now I don't bully,
One day I stopped to think,
And within a single blink,
I realised the wrongs of my ways,
This was the end of my bullying days.

I'm alone now,
We now abide to another bully's rules,
They think us all, to be fools
But I'm alone, with no friends,
When I stopped being a bully, popularity came to an end.

Once I was a bully,
Once I had friends,
But that all came to an end,
Once I was horrid and unfair,
Once I did not show any care.

Once I was a bully!

Inde Gloag Donaldson (11)
St Peter's RC Primary School, Edinburgh

The Five Girls

The five girls
Round the corner they trek,
To the toilets.
I was there
With my friend,
About to leave.
They stopped us in our tracks -
Not letting us leave.

In the playground
There they were,
At the fence -
Giggling away
Whispering and staring at us.

The bell rang
A rush of children running to their lines.
We walked -
The five girls
Pushing past,
Pushing my friend
Right to the ground.
They laughed -
Especially the brunette!

I hated her the most,
She was once my best friend.
But ran off to them -
Turned into one of them.
A bully.

Inside, I knew they were jealous,
Not even friends with each other.
But I knew I was smarter,
Better
And cooler
Than them all put together.

Lauren Goode (11)

St Peter's RC Primary School, Edinburgh

The Bully

There is this new bully at school,
He acts like he's so cool!
His name is Billy,
He causes us pain.
He makes me feel like a fool!

If I tell on him
He bullies me.
But all I want
Is to be free!

I try to ignore it!
I try to have fun!
I just can't bear it!
I have to run!

I don't know if I can take it -
He is driving me crazy!
His name is Billy
He makes us feel silly
We feel like giving up hope!

If I tell on him
He bullies me.
But all I want
Is to be free!

I try to ignore it!
I try to have fun!
I just can't bear it!
I have to run!

We feel like we're giving up freedom.
We need to end your bullying.
We need a solution.
Just for once, Billy,
Please don't be silly!
Join in our games!

John Dunn—Butler (11)
St Peter's RC Primary School, Edinburgh

The Bullies

'The bullies are coming,' I shout,
But why is it
Me being bullied?

They come walking,
Walking, towards me,
As usual.

As they come towards me,
I can hear them shouting,
Shouting at me.

Then suddenly I feel a thud on my back,
As I turn around, I can feel a hand knocking my jaw,
I can feel blood on my face.

I turn around fully and see them there,
I can see them looking smug and happy,
How I hate those bullies.

Then they start whispering to each other,
I get really angry when they do that,
And this time I am going to do something about it.

Then I shout, 'Stop it!'
They look almost startled,
As if they didn't know what to do.

Then to my surprise they turn around and run,
They run to the toilets like babies,
As I stand there shocked.

I turn around and look at everyone staring at me,
They shout to me, 'You have saved us,'
And I just laugh and smile.

Rhona Lilley (11)
St Peter's RC Primary School, Edinburgh

Mission Biscuit

I am cycling down the street
without a peak.
I stop at the nearest house
as quiet as a mouse.
It is all dark as
I stop and park.

I am getting through
a gap in the window,
until I hear a rat-a-tat-tat.
It is okay.
It is safe, I have got
in the kitchen without a sound
as I leap and bound.

I have a look around, yes
I have leapt and bound.
I smell something.
It smells yummy.
I think for a moment,
it smells like biscuits.
I follow that smell,
as I hear a bell.
Oh quick, take the biscuit tin, quickly.
Just in time. I take a look around.

I go through the gap in the window,
I'd better get home quickly
because if I don't
Mum will get suspicious

Elissa Hasson (9)
St Peter's RC Primary School, Edinburgh

The Ghost Bully

The ghost bully
The ghost bully
Is a grizzly bully
He seeks around and around.
The ghost is coming.

He has a ghostly face
One wide mouth to roar and roar
Two skull eyes
And a spiky nose.
The ghost is coming.

He seeks his victim
And there he is
Asleep in the bed
Snoring away.
The ghost is here.

The ghost wakes him up
And in a blink
He shows his ghost face
To startle him.
The ghost is here.

The victim closes his eyes
The ghost is angry
And leaves forever.
The ghost has gone.

Gianluca Rory Cuthbertson (11)
St Peter's RC Primary School, Edinburgh

Mission Biscuit

I tiptoed down the ladder,
as quiet as I could be. I tripped over my
Lego box but no, I did not fall.
I made it to the door and I made it
to the hall and slipped past my sister's room.

I saw a light in the bathroom, *oh no, Mum*
She said, 'Go back to bed and stay there.'
I went back to bed. Minutes passed.
I got out of bed.
I looked in the bathroom. Mum had gone.
I slipped past my sister's bedroom again and I got to the kitchen.

I went to the cupboard and I opened it.
I saw the biscuit box. I took three biscuits, digestives.
I took them and I ate one of them,
It tasted delicious.
I heard someone coming.
I hid in the cupboard and I saw them go.

I ran back to my bed platform,
I ran up the ladder and I thought, *mission complete*.
I ate them and I heard my sister saying, 'Time to get up.'
I thought, *should I tell her? Naahh!*

Joseph Robertson (10)
St Peter's RC Primary School, Edinburgh

Through A Bully's Eyes

I've said goodbye to Mum now and I'm on my way to school
I'm starting to change my attitude as the playground's where I rule
No one dares to tease me or call me a hurtful name
No one dares to tell on me or put my actions to shame.

I have a gang of friends at school
And they're all bullies too
But I'm not a bully inside my heart
I'm scared and that is true.

And now the gang have cornered a boy
He's shaking from head to toe
I suddenly understand his fear
And shout to let him go.

The gang turn round bewildered
And skulk away in shame
I will no longer bully kids
It is no longer my game.

I'm now a grown man and have a daughter and a son
But I still feel bad inside myself for everything I've done
I warn both my children from the bottom of my heart
Never turn to bullying, it's addictive when you start.

Christopher David Turnbull (12)
St Peter's RC Primary School, Edinburgh

Why Am I Being Bullied?

Here I am again -
Back in the school grounds.
Ready to be beaten,
Beaten with a sound.

I can see them coming . . .
Getting closer every time.
Struggling to run away,
To buy myself some time.

How do they do it?
Hurt me every day,
Going home with bruises,
To waste me all away.

I hate it that I hate them,
They taunt me - they tease me.
I want them to release me,
Please, oh please believe me!

It's the last day,
I hope they go away.
Please - *help me!*

Katie O'Brien (11)
St Peter's RC Primary School, Edinburgh

Gone Forever

I was in a dream,
Me, Mum, hiding under the floorboards,
The Nazis found us and took us to a camp.

Little children, teenagers, adults,
Every one of them suffering,
No food, no water, no life.

Rounded up into groups,
'Shave your heads, wear these clothes!'
The Nazis demanded.

Be 'their' slaves, do 'their' work,
March in a crowd,
Till the end when we reached the point.

The point where people stood,
One by one, until they were killed,
Gassed, shot, gone forever.

The dream had ended -
One day this dream happened to me,
Gassed, shot, gone forever.

Francesca Faichney (11)
St Peter's RC Primary School, Edinburgh

Stop Racism Now!

Stop racism now, it's bad,
It makes me sad.
Stop racism now, it's bad
And it makes me mad,
Stop it now.

I hate it now, just stop it,
It does not matter, black or white, who cares?
It's just the human race
I know what it feels like
It's sad, I hate it.

Just wait there, who cares,
We should be nice,
Black or white, it does not matter,
Stop! Stop! Stop!
It's bad, it's sad, don't do it!

It's bad, I hate it,
It's so annoying, stop racism now,
I hate it, it stops now!

Robbie Keane (9)
St Peter's RC Primary School, Edinburgh

Stop Racism!

Why should you be racist?
Think it is cool?
It happens a lot, especially in school.
Why should you be racist?
Think it'll make you tough?
Well you shouldn't do it anymore,
You'll end up in handcuffs.

Racism is wrong and very, very cruel,
Stop right now,
You're acting like a fool
Racism is wrong, stop it now!
It's not a talent
No need to take a bow.

Racism is not nice, it makes people sad
Lots of people do it but it's very, very bad.
Racism is not nice, so *stop it now!*
And if you call people names
You'll cause a big row.

Adele Pacitti (9)
St Peter's RC Primary School, Edinburgh

Why Me?

Why me?
Why me, who was punched and kicked?
Was it because of my name?
Why me, who was ignored and had no friends?
Was it because of my clothes?
Why me, whose money was stolen
And was called names?
Was it because of what I liked
Or where I was from?
No.
It's none of those,
It's my skin colour.
That's why I'm punched, kicked and called names,
But that stopped a long time ago
Because I told someone
And I stood up to them
And now they have learned their lesson.
That we are all the same.

Matthew Messer (11)
St Peter's RC Primary School, Edinburgh

Red Card For Racism

Racism is bad and it makes people sad.
You can stop if you try
Keep racism out
And unhappiness in all can be stopped.

Racism, racism, stop it now
So that they can be welcome in every town.
Why are we racist?
We don't know.
Is it funny?
I don't think so!

You can say no and show you can help.
You know racism is wrong
But you have to stay strong.
Racism makes people mad
Also it is very bad.
Show racism the red card today
And make someone's day!

Claire Wong (9)
St Peter's RC Primary School, Edinburgh

Stand Up To Hatred

Why was Hitler so cruel?
To treat Jews like fools,
And send them to death camps,
Not even letting them choose.

Why were they gassed?
Their population crashed,
They were starved as well,
It must have felt like Hell.

While this was happening
The Allies were fighting back,
Trying to overcome the Nazis,
And get all the Jews back.

Poems like this will help us remember,
Why the Nazis had to surrender,
Because they were so unkind,
It affected the whole of mankind.

Brendan Mullan (11)
St Peter's RC Primary School, Edinburgh

Stop Racism Now

Racism is bad, it makes people sad.
It's not cool, the bullies think they rule.
They are so bad, they make me sad.

They should feel ashamed, but they feel famed.
The range of the world is not that people should change.
Speak up about racism!

Marcus Corrigan (9)
St Peter's RC Primary School, Edinburgh

This Nightmare

As I walk into the playground
I feel fear
I look around for the bully
But she is not there.

As I walk up to my friend
I see the bully
Suddenly she sees me
She can see me fully.

I scurry away
Like a little mouse
With fear in my heart
I run back to my house.

I slam my door shut
And I realise no one cares
This will never end
Not this nightmare.

Daniella McGinley (11)
St Peter's RC Primary School, Edinburgh

There Is A Boy In Our Class . . .

There is a boy in our class
and no one really likes him.

There is a boy in our class
that we used to tease and taunt.

There is a boy in our class
and he has had troubles at home.

There is a boy in our class
that people won't talk to.

There is a boy in our class
who doesn't have a bed to sleep in.

There is a boy in our class
and now he teases us.

There is a boy in the class
and we made him the bully.

Patrick Mulvanny (11)
St Peter's RC Primary School, Edinburgh

Racism Stops Now!

Racism, it's really bad,
And to be fair, it drives me mad.
It sometimes happens all the time,
But let's be honest, it is a crime.
Some people are black, some people are white,
But technically neither are wrong or right.
The problem is the human race,
It's sad to say but that's the case.
But think about it, black and white,
There's not much difference, they're both right.
So what's the point in being mean?
To beat this monster, work as a team.

The message in this poem,
I'm trying to make it clear,
That racism, it's never right
And help is always near.

Francis Gill (9)
St Peter's RC Primary School, Edinburgh

Racism Is Bad

Racism is always found
at least once on country ground.
We need to throw racism out
of our country and our school,
it's just not cool.
Racism just makes me want to shout.
Why do people treat one another bad
because of their skin colour?
It's not their fault they're black, brown or white,
you can talk to them, it's not like they're going to bite.
Why can't people just be nice?
Racist people should pay the price.
Always remember
you should know racism isn't good.
So why do people do it?
You know it will just turn out bad.

Jack Donaldson (10)
St Peter's RC Primary School, Edinburgh

Why Are Some People Racist?

Why do people, black and brown
Get punched and kicked and thrown down?
Why do people that believe in different things
Get treated as if they are different beings?

Why do people call other people racist names?
I think racist people are just like a group of angry cranes

Show racism the red card and lend people a helping hand!

Lewis Mazzei (10)
St Peter's RC Primary School, Edinburgh

The Red Card's Out

The red card's out
The crowd scream and shout
For what has been done
For we are throwing racism out.

Different ways, bad days
We can't have room for this
It's not our fault if we're different
Imagine if the world was all the same
There would be no spice
And then the world would have to pay the price.

That's my say
I hope one day
That racism can move on
Then we could have a good life again
Then racism would be gone!

Ruth Anne Dolan (9)
St Peter's RC Primary School, Edinburgh

The Racist Monster

If you let the racist monster get in your way,
Then it will affect your life and you will have to pay!

The monster starts off hurting and then it becomes agony,
So we together have to stop this monster and tell him, 'Go away!'

We have to fight this monster and stamp him out of this place,
I hope you agree with me because I need the help of the
whole human race

James Stuart Rennie (9)
St Peter's RC Primary School, Edinburgh

The Sad Story Of Racism

Why, oh why am I to blame?
It really is such a shame
Why do people treat me differently
Just because my skin is brown and not creamy?

But I will hold my head high
And look up into the sky
I'm dreaming of a day when people will just walk by
And leave me alone to try, try, try.

I get teased, attacked and punched in the back
Why do I get treated like this
Just because I come from Iraq?
But oh why are people so cruel?
Don't they know they're breaking school rules?
But if racism stopped it would be the perfect school
Show racism the red card!

Ross Mark Purves
St Peter's RC Primary School, Edinburgh

The Big Bullies

Look,
Here they come.
The bullies,
Always mean
All the time.

They come,
Closer
And closer.
I stand up,
Walk backwards.

The bullies stopped.
I told them to go away.
They were shocked!
They went away . . .
And never bullied me again!

Yasmin Mair (11)

St Peter's RC Primary School, Edinburgh

Mission Biscuit

From my bed, down the ladder
I go through my messy room as slow as a slug
But *oh no!* I step on a squeaker. My brother wakes.
I say, 'Come on let's raid the biscuit tin.'

We reach the kitchen now
Chris and I look for the tin,
We look top to bottom
'Shush!' I said, 'be as quiet as a mouse.
Aha it's the tin, let's dig in.'

We reach in and take some biscuits
'Let's go get out of here, do not wake Matty or we are busted.'
So back we go to the room.
'Mission complete, let's just eat them.'
Yum! they were really nice!
I say to Chris, 'Let's not leave any evidence.'

Nicholas Dolan (10)
St Peter's RC Primary School, Edinburgh

Standing Up

Ha! I have him now,
He's got nowhere to run and nowhere to hide -
He's stuck in that corner.
What's this,
He's walking towards me,
Is he going to stand up to me?
He is!
He's standing up to me.
Now, I've got nowhere to run or to hide.
'Please . . .
I beg you please,
Don't tell on me!'
'I have you bully!
Say it - say you are sorry.'
'I am sorry.'

Finlay MacKenzie (11)
St Peter's RC Primary School, Edinburgh

Stop Racism!

Racism is found everywhere around,
You can find it in school and in the swimming pool.
It is very sad, it makes people mad.

It has to stop,
It is going over the top
It will turn into a fight and that's not right.
Let's stop now!
Show racism the red card!

Emily Ireland (9)
St Peter's RC Primary School, Edinburgh

Stop It

Stop bullying
That girl
What has she done?
It is not her fault
That she is as dumb as a mouse
Making her sad
Is just not fair
She tries her
Hardest each day
She is getting better
Even look, she is getting good grades
If you let her be
She will be OK
So please stop it
Is that OK?

Melissa Scott (11)

St Peter's RC Primary School, Edinburgh

Stop Racism Now!

Racism is bad, it makes people sad.
The person who does it is obviously mad.
But don't take your anger out in an upsetting way.
One important message: don't let it lay.
Pick it up quickly and chuck it away.

Dispose of it soon before it gets free
Don't let it ruin your friendship between you and me!

But what is the difference between black and white skin?
And when I see it I feel really dim.

It's bad in all ways
Don't let it go on for loads of days.
Stop it on day one,
Please don't let it go on.

Eilidh Buchan (9)
St Peter's RC Primary School, Edinburgh

Stop Racism Now!

Racism is bad, it makes people sad
They get angry and it's very bad
Give them a chance, it makes people mad.

Don't make a fight because I'm white
Look left, look right
Everywhere is black or white.

Some people don't even care
People who do it are unfair
Big shame, they will have to change.

Evan Cole (9)
St Peter's RC Primary School, Edinburgh

No More Racism!

Racism is a crime, you can go to jail
So don't try it, your plan will fail
When I'm getting bullied, I run off and cry
When I should really tell someone, I need to try.

I am South African
And people tease me about it
I thought they were my friends
But now I really doubt it.

Racism is everywhere
Because it's in the air
And we all have to stop it!
Our friends may encourage us
But we know we have to stop.

Mhairi-Claire McGowan (9)
St Peter's RC Primary School, Edinburgh

Don't Be Racist

When someone is racist, I start to see red,
When someone is racist it makes them
Sad, scared, unhappy, angry
Why are people racist?
Skin colour doesn't matter.

Don't be racist, it is horrible
Don't be racist, it is mean
Racism is bad, it makes me sad
Stop being racist!

Mairi Mulvanny (9)
St Peter's RC Primary School, Edinburgh

Run

The victim

Nearer and nearer,
The bullies are really near.
Walking then running,
Away from all the bullies,
Away from this stupid school.

The bully

What is she doing?
She is such a big coward.
Then suddenly she turns
And says, 'Go away now!'
I turn around and *run, run!*

Rachel Brooks (11)
St Peter's RC Primary School, Edinburgh

Stop Racism Now!

Racism is nothing bright,
Everyone is black or white,
Please don't start a fight,
Because you might be black,
And I might be white.

Racism is super bad
That's why it makes me sad.
Please can you make it stop?
Because it's a horrible plot.

Xavier Laird (9)
St Peter's RC Primary School, Edinburgh

The Victim And His Bully

Victim

A big fit bully
Comes marching down towards me -
Not again I think,
I must stand up to him here!
Tell the teacher what I fear.

Bully

There he is at last!
That boy who is popular -
Why can't I be him?
Then maybe I'd have some friends!
Is fighting the way for me?

David McLauchlan (10)
St Peter's RC Primary School, Edinburgh

One Man

It was because of one man - just one single man,
That the Holocaust had to have happened.
It was because of one man – one horrible man,
That the Jewish race had to be flattened.

But if it was just one man - just one single man,
Why couldn't the Jews just say *no*?
Because he controlled nearly all of Europe
And he forced all the Jews just to go.

So if this happens just one more time,
We can't let one man cause this pain.
And back down in Poland, where Auschwitz camp lies,
There are two words: *never again*.

Rory Doherty (11)
St Peter's RC Primary School, Edinburgh

Why Be Racist?

Why be racist? Is it cool?
It happens everywhere, even in a swimming pool
Being racist is not funny, you're being a fool.

Racism is not fair, why make fun of what people wear?
On their hair or on their face,
Why be racist?

If you are being racist, stop and think
Do you want your heart to be as cold as an ice rink?
So stop to think before you have no friends.

So stop racism now and make St Peter's proud.

Lauren Service (9)
St Peter's RC Primary School, Edinburgh

Stop Racism Now!

Racism is so very bad,
It makes people very sad,
In fact it makes me really mad
It doesn't matter if you're from Chad!

Racism is so very cruel,
Especially if you're from Peru!
Racism is not nice at all
Especially if you're from Nepal!

Your skin colour does not matter
Racism is very scattered
Racism is everywhere
People really should care!

Jack Gromett (9)
St Peter's RC Primary School, Edinburgh

Racism

Racism is terrible,
Racism is wrong,
Racism will hurt people
Cos racism is strong.

How would you feel
If that were you?
You wouldn't like it,
They wouldn't too.

You need to be strong
And say no to your friends,
Stand up to racists,
Until racism ends.

Orla Fitzgerald (10)
St Peter's RC Primary School, Edinburgh

Racism Stops Now

Racism is bad, it makes people sad
Black skin, white skin, brown skin
It doesn't matter, it is only what they are
On the inside that we care about.

Everybody should get treated the same
Nobody should get the blame
For black, brown or white
If we don't stop now this could get into a fight.

It's not fair, it's not right
Racism has to stop now before the night!
Show people that you care by showing racism the red card!
We can make a big difference!

Kimberley Anderson (9)
St Peter's RC Primary School, Edinburgh

Kick Racism Out Of The World

Racism is not good
We should really get it out
But when it's all around
We just want to kick it out.

It doesn't matter if they're white, black or brown
Let's just not do it in our country, in our town.
Racism should be stopped
No one should like racism, no one should be shot.

Religion doesn't matter either
Everyone should be your friend
So let's kick racism out of the world and be everybody's friend.
Show racism the red card!

Michael Duffy (9)
St Peter's RC Primary School, Edinburgh

Christmas Acrostic

C rackers are loud as they go *bang* ·
H o, *ho, ho!* Says a big, fat man
R udolph flies up high in the sky
I cicles melting; *drip, drip, drip*
S anta packs up and away he goes
T ime for some visits to children he knows
M erry Christmas to everyone
A nd happy times with friends one and all
S omeone to give to, friends far and near

Merry Christmas and a happy new year.

Brook Chandler (7)
Sheuchan Primary School, Stranraer

A Rainforest Journey

Giant anteaters roam the floor,
You can find so much more.
In the understorey jaguars hide,
Above the treetops beautiful birds glide.
In the canopy creatures stay still,
Beautiful lizards have a frill.
On the floor there are fruits,
In the treetops monkeys hoot.
In the emergents scarlet macaws fly,
In the rainforest animals cry.
In the day stick insects sleep,
On the floor tree frogs leap.
Baby jaguar don't you worry,
Daddy will be back in a hurry.

Gordon Forbes (7)

Sheuchan Primary School, Stranraer

Rainforest Creatures

Snakes slide
Monkeys hide
Birds slide
Spiders hide
Trees grow
Sloths slow
Butterflies flitter
Flitter and pose
Tapir with a great big nose.

Jade Blair (7)

Sheuchan Primary School, Stranraer

Untitled

On the dark and gloomy floor,
There are bugs and so much more.
On the floor you will find,
Snakes and bugs of any kind.
In the understorey creatures hide,
Above the treetops birds will glide.
In the emergent you hear birds cheep,
Trying their best to have a sleep.
Little bird, don't you worry,
Daddy will be back in a hurry.
Baby bird, don't you cry,
Mummy bird will fly on by.

Ashlyn Kinahan (7)
Sheuchan Primary School, Stranraer

The Dark And Gloomy Forest Floor

On the dark and gloomy floor,
There are snakes and so much more.
In the canopy monkeys leap,
So much fun they fall asleep.
Giant anteaters always hide,
Birds and parrots like to glide.
The jaguar is scurrying fast,
Night-time will soon be past,
On the dark and gloomy forest floor.

Lewis McCamon (7)
Sheuchan Primary School, Stranraer

Christmas Acrostic

C rackers are loud
H olly is prickly
R udolph is happy
I cicles are cold
S nowmen melt
T urkey is tasty
M istletoe is magical
A ngels are mysterious
S anta's super sleigh.

Cameron Miller (7)
Sheuchan Primary School, Stranraer

Rainforest At Night

Creatures hide and birds glide
Monkeys roar and waterfalls pour
Jaguars sleep up high in the trees
They do not frighten me!
Snakes slither on the floor
Jaguars wake up and roar
The emergents are big and tall
Raindrops fall and fall . . . and fall.

Ryan McGhie (8)
Sheuchan Primary School, Stranraer

The Rainforest

Deep down on the forest floor,
There are snakes and so much more.
Little tiny beasts will scurry,
Always seems to be in a hurry.
In the canopy creatures hide,
Every kind of bird can glide.
Creatures looking for a kill,
Soon at night all will be still.

Trinity Newell (7)
Sheuchan Primary School, Stranraer

A Jungle Journey

On the forest floor creatures are leaping
Deep down inside some are sleeping
In the understorey creatures can hide
Up in the treetops birds can glide
In the forest are wonderful creatures
And so much more!

Sophie Robertson (7)
Sheuchan Primary School, Stranraer

Rainforests

On the dark and gloomy floor,
Lots of bugs and so much more.
On treetops tall, creatures sleep,
Open their eyes to take a peep.
In the treetops monkeys swing
Branch to branch, oh, what a din!

Finn Onori (7)

Sheuchan Primary School, Stranraer

Cinquain

Slimy
Crawling onward
Looking out for lizards
Slithering through the forest floor
The snake.

Niall Slavin (7)

Sheuchan Primary School, Stranraer

Dinosaur Opposites

Dinosaur happy, dinosaur sad,
Dinosaur good and dinosaur bad,
Dinosaur high, dinosaur low,
Dinosaur above and dinosaur below.

Callum Lees (7)

Sheuchan Primary School, Stranraer

The Jaguar – Haiku

Lovely jaguar
Pretty coat with painted spots
Hunting in the trees.

Sean Edgar (7)
Sheuchan Primary School, Stranraer

Butterfly – Haiku

Flutter through the air
Spreading rainbows in the sky
Resting on the tree.

Emma Smith (7)
Sheuchan Primary School, Stranraer

Beautiful Butterfly – Haiku

Stunning butterfly,
Lovely butterfly flies by,
Such attractive wings.

Dawn Wyllie (7)
Sheuchan Primary School, Stranraer

Homecoming Scotland 2009

Scotland, bonnie old Scotland
Where can I start?
Weather, flowers, landscape
I try to remember

Whit about the weather?
Dull,
Grey,
Black,
Rain,
Clouds,
Nae much sun,
I try to remember

Whit about the flowers?
Heather,
Foxgloves,
Daffodils,
Nae much else,
I try to remember

Whit about the landscape?
Mountains as high as the eye can see
Lakes
Ma house
Nae much else,
I remember it now

Going back all the years
Tae the Langtoun - Kirkcaldy
Tae my house
Tae see the flowers
Tae see the landscape
Oh, I wish I was in
Bonnie Scotland.

Jordan Hamilton (9)
Sinclairtown Primary School, Kirkcaldy

Where Did They Come From?

The Scottish ale,
The Irn Bru,
The whisky,
Where did they all come from?

The haggis,
The neeps,
The tatties,
Where did they all come from?

The thistle,
The lavender,
The heather,
Where did they all come from?

Amy McDonald,
Red Hot Chilli Peppers,
The Proclaimers,
Where did they all come from?

Scotland Today,
Taggart,
River City,
Where did they all come from?

Caledonia,
Scotia,
Bonnie Scotland,
That's where they all come from!

Denny Miller (9)
Sinclairtown Primary School, Kirkcaldy

Up In The Highlands

Up in the Highlands,
There are old, demolished castles
And in the misty lakes there's a
Loch Ness monster.

Up and down,
Round and round,
Scaring all the fish.

All the haggises going to the abattoir,
Getting killed.
The emerald-green landscapes,
Jaggy thistles all around.

Bag pipers playing Scottish tunes,
Everybody shouting, 'Wiptae doo!'

Highlanders. Believe you me,
They have no pants on.
That's how they scare their enemies!
They risk their lives, just for us.

I am true Scottish
And I'm proud of it!

Jack Smith (9)
Sinclairtown Primary School, Kirkcaldy

Why Am I Scottish?

Why is ma mum Scottish?
Why is ma mum's mum Scottish?
Why am I Scottish?
Why am I not French?

Why is haggis called haggis?
Why was William Wallace a knight?
And why, if you speak Scottish,
Do you say nicht instead of night?

Why is a Highland coo hairy?
Why do bagpipes sound loud?
Why is Gordon Ramsay scary?
And why am I so proud?

Why is ma dad Scottish?
Why is ma dad's dad Scottish?
Why am I Scottish?
Why am I not French?

Kieran McCallum (9)
Sinclairtown Primary School, Kirkcaldy

Haggis

Up in the Highlands there's a thing called
A haggis.
It roams free day and night
And plays tricks on the hunters.

You could say it's like a tiny cow.
It's a wee, fuzzy creature
And has a tiny elephant's trunk
For sooking up food.

It speaks in a Gaelic accent
And moos when its scared.
It listens to bagpipe music
And dances in the moonlight.

So when you're eating haggis,
Don't forget to listen for the bagpipes,
Look for the fuzzy trunk
And imagine the moonlight.

Ben Clark (9)
Sinclairtown Primary School, Kirkcaldy

The Lonely Piper

I'm the piper who nobody cares about,
I get left out no matter what.
The clouds and shadows may cover me,
But I don't care.

They bullied me until I was black and blue,
Bruised and battered.
I don't matter to the world,
Not compared to them.

I travel home over the long Scottish bridge,
On my own with no one to talk to,
Back to my sobbing, grieving mother.
'Be more like your father,' she says.

My father was a fighter and so should I be.
I try not to think about him too much.
I stand out from the crowd
And I am known.

Abbie Keillor (9)
Sinclairtown Primary School, Kirkcaldy

The Scottish Invention Capsule

I put in the capsule
A fizzy bottle of Irn Bru,
A glass of tasty whisky,
A tub of marmalade that tastes so sweet.

I put in the capsule
A film of Peter Pan that looks so good,
My favourite golf ball,
A cord of a ringing telephone.

I put in the capsule
An antique picture of Robert Burns,
A happy song of Amy McDonald,
A hair of a barking Scottish terrier.

I put in the capsule
A scale of a Loch Ness monster,
A work of art from Charles Rennie Mackintosh,
I put in the capsule a taste of Scotland.

Annie Simpson (9)
Sinclairtown Primary School, Kirkcaldy

The Tour Bus

'Welcome aboard my tour bus!

In Fife you will see Ravenscraig Castle,
We will be visiting Starks Park
And stopping at Leven chip shop,
Let's have a toilet break in Kirkcaldy!

Hold onto your hats as we cross the Forth Road Bridge,
Welcome to Edinburgh, our next stop is Edinburgh Dungeons,
The rides will be so deafening it will spike up your hair!
Our last stop is to the castle - listen for the cannons.

We are now at the end of our journey,
We will be serving Irn Bru and shortbread.
Enjoy the refreshments, here are our special guests -
The Proclaimers!

Thank you for your custom. I hope you enjoyed your journey.'

Scott Anderson (9)
Sinclairtown Primary School, Kirkcaldy

The Annoying Scots Child

Dad, does a golf ball have a face?
Dad, does a golf club tell you how far the ball goes?
Dad, when you hit the grass with the golf club, does it hurt?

Dad, can I drink whisky?
Dad, does sister get to drink whisky?
Dad, can I go and feed the cat whisky?

Dad, can I ride on the Loch Ness monster?
Dad, can I feed the Loch Ness monster?
Dad, can I brush the Loch Ness monster's teeth?

Dad, can I drink a whole bottle of Irn Bru?
Dad, does Irn Bru turn you into Peter Pan?
Dad, can I give the cat Irn Bru?
No!

Gillian Ness (9)
Sinclairtown Primary School, Kirkcaldy

The Scottish Landscape

I can see . . .
The swishing oak trees,
The white, snowy mountains
And the lovely Scottish thistles.

I can hear . . .
The lovely, musical bagpipes,
The birds singing gratefully
And the dancing waves of the lake.

I can smell . . .
The wonderful lodges smelling of haggis,
The magnificence of the Scottish breeze
And the astonishing seaweed of the Loch Ness.

That's why I think it's beautiful.

Louie Cruickshank (9)
Sinclairtown Primary School, Kirkcaldy

Irn Bru

Why is Irn Bru orange?
I wonder?
What is it made out of?
I wonder?

Is it made of fizzy gas?
Is there some orange juice in it?

Did Rabbie Burns drink it?
Or maybe even William Wallace?
I wonder?

When was it first made?
I wonder?
The taste is . . .
Barry, pure brilliant and braw!

Callum Foote (9)

Sinclairtown Primary School, Kirkcaldy

Scotland Is My Home

I love to be in Scotland
It makes me feel at home.
The hills, the air,
The bonnie, grey sky.

Scotland is my home.
It's the only place I want to be.
Scotland loves me so.

When I come home from abroad,
I feel the cold,
Then I know I am home.
I know, I know.

Scotland is my home.

Louise Carr (9)
Sinclairtown Primary School, Kirkcaldy

A Poem For Irn Bru

Oh, Irn Bru is fizzing all day,
Even when I hit the hay,
Irn Bru so sparkly orange,
Drink it while eating an orange.

Oh, Irn Bru,
I'm glad Scotland made you.
Oh, Irn Bru, fizzing over a barricade,
Better than orangeade.

And now we're here,
In my hand.
Oh, Irn Bru,
I love you.

Steven Trantham (9)
Sinclairtown Primary School, Kirkcaldy

Young Writers Information

We hope you have enjoyed reading this book - and that you will continue to enjoy it in the coming years.

If you like reading and writing poetry drop us a line, or give us a call, and we'll send you a free information pack.

Alternatively if you would like to order further copies of this book or any of our other titles, then please give us a call or log onto our website at www.youngwriters.co.uk

Young Writers Information
Remus House
Coltsfoot Drive
Peterborough
PE2 9JX
(01733) 890066